RIDING *the* CRESTS of MURDERS

ERNEST SALOTTI

First paperback edition published by Page Publishing 2022
Second paperback edition published by Ernest Salotti 2025

ISBN 979-8-99135-891-0 (paperback)
ISBN 979-8-88654-520-3 (digital)

Printed in the USA by Village Books

C H A P T E R   1

———

THE BLINDSIDE

Private Detective Dickson Diamond had just returned to his office after a long night staking out a woman and her lover in an upscale motel next to the Bellingham International Airport.

He walked over to the coat rack behind his chair and hung his jacket and shoulder holster. Tired from a long night, he sat down in his warm leather chair, placing his feet up on his desk to catch a nap before his partner came to work.

He pulled his hat down over his face and chuckled at the thought of a person being so tired after sitting on his ass all night just to get the pictures of the two lovers leaving the motel as they split up and went to their respective home and loving spouses.

Detective Diamond hated working on these kinds of contracts. There was always big trouble, and he was in the middle. But he needed the money to pay the rent.

He had just closed his eyes when a loud banging on the office door shocked him. He dropped his feet to the floor and pulled his .357 revolver from his shoulder holster and waited to see what was coming.

There was another loud hammering on the door.

"Come in! The door's unlocked!" Diamond shouted as he slid his .357 under a newspaper on the desk.

As he watched he knew some poor bastard was coming through the door to shoot him for stalking his wife.

The door opened slowly, and an older, well-dressed woman stood in the doorway and for a moment, she looked around the office, then walked in.

Dick noticed a big shadow behind her; it was a huge man trailing.

"What can I do for you, miss?" Dick asked.

The woman said nothing. She walked over to Dick's desk and sat on a chair across from him while the huge man stood behind her.

Dick watched her adjust her dress as she glanced over his pictures and awards hanging on the wall behind him.

"Make yourself comfortable, and if you can find time, tell me how I can help you?" Dick asked sarcastically.

"Don't be a smart-ass detective, just listen to me," the lady stated.

"I'm sorry," Dick replied.

"Well, detective, the police have stopped looking for my sweet daughter, who has been missing for weeks. I believe they ran out of leads and have given up on finding her. I need you to find her," the woman stated.

"Let's back up and try to understand who we are. You know my name, and who I am, that's written on the door. But I don't know who you are or that big fellow behind you," Dick stated firmly.

"I'm Peggy Powers, and this man behind me is my son Gene Powers. He stays close to me after a car wreck, which left him to be a little slow mentally. Now can I get on with my story about my daughter?"

"If it's an investigation you want, I can't help you, I have other investigations," Dick explained.

"Look, Dick, by the way, where did you get a name like Dick," Peggy asked?

Before Dick could respond, Peggy spoke up again. "Dick, I don't give a shit about your other jobs. I need to find my daughter, and I will do what I have to do to find her, even if it means Gene pulling your arm off and beating your damn head off with the bloody ends," Peggy stated with anger.

Dick looked over and up at Gene. Then commented, "Since you put it that way, I'll do what I can to help. But the police will do a great job in finding missing persons. Is it possible she may have just left with a friend?"

"Okay, Detective Diamond, listen to me, I can keep Gene under control if I see you are truly trying to find my girl. If you don't, Gene will rip you apart like a rag doll," Peggy said again with the same anger.

"Okay, Peggy, I believe you. Tell me about your daughter and the day she went missing. I need her full name, a picture of her, and the names of her friends and enemies. Do not leave out anyone. If you hide or cover up anyone, I will stop investigating, and Gene can rip me apart," Dick clarified.

Peggy agreed to Dick's terms and told him about Jamie Lee Powers, a blue-eyed blonde nineteen-year-old weighing 140 pounds and standing five feet and five inches tall. The only outstanding feature is a rose tattoo on her left shoulder. Her main love and hobby is computers; she studies computers at the university.

"Now tell me about her friends and enemies. Did she have a break up with her boyfriend," Dick questioned.

"She has no enemies and only one good friend that I know of, a boy by the name of Bodie White. He is like Jamie, crazy about computers."

"Before we go any further, I need you to read and sign this contract. This contract will give me the right to receive a copy of the police reports," Dick said.

"Sure, give me the contract, I'll sign it, so you will get to work," Peggy responded.

"Thanks, Mrs. Powers, now all I need is a retainer," Dick stated.

"I've got the retainer, so don't get your shorts in a wad, Dick."

After she signed the contract, Peggy got up to leave and Dick said, "Peggy, I'll pick up the police report on Jamie and call you when I have news."

Peggy tossed an envelope on Dick's desk and said, "I will expect a call from you daily, Dick."

Peggy turned and walked out with Gene trailing right behind her.

Diamond didn't pick up the envelope; instead, he poured himself a shot of brandy and downed it to relieve the stress after Peggy's demanding discussions and that long night.

After another brandy, Dick decided to open the envelope and slowly dumped the contents out on the desk. Peggy had left a card with her information printed on it and $5,000 cash.

That's a good retainer, Dick thought as he replaced the money and card in the envelope and then dropped it in a desk drawer.

Dick's partner, Martha (Marty) Mills, walked in and placed her coffee cup on her desk, and asked, "What's with the lady and the big ape behind her leaving the office?"

"That was Peggy and her son. She is looking for her daughter. The police ran out of leads, and she thinks they have given up finding her daughter. Now, she wants us to keep looking," Dick explained.

"What are you going to do, we're full of cases?"

Dick handed Marty the envelope from the desk and said Peggy had left it on his desk.

Marty opened the envelope and asked, "What's with this cash?"

"That is the retainer, I had to take Peggy's contract, or she'd have her mentally slow son Gene break my neck," Dick explained.

Marty dropped the money back into the desk drawer and said, "Let's go eat and talk about it."

At breakfast at Diamond Jim's Restaurant, Marty commented, "This is going to be a hard case. Jamie is an adult, and she can go wherever she likes."

"Marty, I took the case to get Peggy out of our office and bring us much-needed money. But above those reasons, I hate that a young woman was taken for the benefit of others," Dick said as he paid the restaurant check.

After breakfast, they stopped by the sheriff's office to pick up a copy of Jamie's case and informed the investigating detective they would be working for Mrs. Powers.

While in the detective division, they met Detective Paul Meeks of the San Juan County Sheriff's Office, who's in charge of Jamie's case and was happy to help them in their investigation.

"Marty, it looks like someone else wants to get Peggy out of their office," Dick commented in a low voice.

Detective Meeks gave them all the reports he could, and said he would have an office in the Whatcom County Sheriff's office while the investigation was going on. He then wished them good luck in finding Jamie; he would help when he could.

Back in the car, as he drove toward Jamie's apartment to start their investigation, Marty stated, "We have little information to go on." Then she cited a few facts she found in the reports Detective Meeks had given them.

"What did you find in the reports to give us some guidance, Marty," Dick asked?

"Here's what jumped out to me," Marty explained. "One, Jamie is a leader in the Western Washington University computers studies, and she will finish her degree this year. Two, Jamie was on a camping trip on Orcus Island, where she went missing along with her friend Bodie White. Three, the sheriff found Jamie and her friend's camping gear still at the campsite and it had been used. Four, the two are of age and could have just left, but there are no signs of that, her car was still at the scene. Five, the two are low profile, and they don't belong to any group. Six, Jamie has no affiliation with any known drugs or crime organizations, nor does she use drugs. Seven, the two have part-time jobs to cover their expenses, and they are not in debt. Dick, this girl and her friend are squeaky clean."

Dick thought for a time, then said, "That's right, Marty, because she is squeaky clean, is the reason I'm worried. There is a simple answer for their disappearance, or this is a professional kill for an unknown reason."

"Why would anyone want to kill those two," Marty asked?

"The two missing people are clean, no money problems or crimes. The crime scene was clean, and nothing was taken, not even her car. There are two items I didn't see in the police report, their laptops and phones. They would never go anywhere without their laptops or cell phones," Dick said.

"If that is the case, these people we are looking for could be deadly to us," Marty responded.

"We may be walking into a lion's den with nothing but a stick," Dick explained.

"I sure hope not."

Nothing was said about the case until they arrived at a small house on a dead-end street just outside of the university: a house Jamie had recently moved to.

"This is the place," Dick said as he pointed to the blue police tape still on the door.

Dick pulled into the driveway and got out with Marty.

"There's a person coming out of the house, she must be cleaning the house for new renters," Dick commented.

The woman came up to Marty and Dick and asked, "Are you here to rent the house? I'm the owner, Maggy Lee Justice."

Dick introduced himself and Marty to the owner and said they were working with the police on the missing lady, Jamie, who rented this house. Then Dick asked about Jamie's visitors and activities.

The owner said a couple of people visited Jamie. Once a week, a woman would come and stay for ten minutes, then leave. As to why this woman came, she didn't know. The other person was her close friend Bodie White who came over all the time.

Dick thanked the owner, and the two started walking back to their car when the owner spoke up, "There was one other item. The woman drove a new black BMW that students couldn't afford."

Dick again thanked her, and the two started canvassing the streets where Jamie lived. They needed a lead to Jamie's disappearance.

By the end of the day of hard canvassing, the two found nothing.

CHAPTER 2

WHERE DO WE GO FROM HERE?

Back at the office, Dick started to open the office door and found it ajar. He pulled his gun and slowly pushed the door open. He looked over the offices and found the rooms clean, and the secretary was gone.

With the offices clear, Marty stated, "This is the time the secretary goes home. I will call and see if she is there."

Dick checked the money Peggy left and found it still in the drawer, but the card with Peggy's information was gone.

"Was the card the only item taken?" Marty said.

"It looks that way. Why would a person go to the trouble of jimmying the office door, and only take the card," Dick questioned?

From the looks of this place, they didn't find what they were after.

"Go home, Marty, I'll straighten up here," Dick suggested.

After Marty left Dick straightened up the office and then left to find a place to eat before continuing his work.

The next morning, Dick was back in the office waiting for Marty.

Marty was running late, and she didn't answer her phone.

Dick stopped waiting and headed to Marty's place.

At her home, Dick found the front door ajar. Knowing Marty lived alone, he called the Bellingham Police to check out the house.

Dick wanted to go into the house to make sure his partner was not in a life-threatening situation, but he didn't.

Within two minutes, the police had the house covered, and the lead officer, along with one other uniformed officer, entered the front door with their weapons out, and Dick followed.

The lead officer shouted, "*Police, we're coming in.*"

There was no response.

The three entered and quickly swept the first-floor areas.

The officers moved up the stairs slowly to the second floor. They searched and didn't find Marty.

As the officers started to clear the house, Dick asked, "Did anyone check the basement?"

"I didn't know there was a basement, where is the door," one officer stated?

"It's by the refrigerator, it's hard to see," Dick said.

One of the uniformed officers led the way down the stairs to the basement followed by another officer with Dick trailing closely behind. Their gun barrels quickly moving to areas of darkness. Once in the basement, they spread out to search the dim-lit areas. At an unused coal shute, Dick found Marty.

She was lying on her back with blood oozing from her chest and shoulder.

"I found Marty! She is over here," Dick bellowed out as he pulled her lifeless body out of the shute and onto the floor!

Before Dick could check Marty's pulse, the other uniformed officers were by his side to help.

"She has a pulse, call an aid unit! We've got to get her to the hospital and quick," Dick commanded.

Within minutes, the aid unit was there and worked to save Marty's life as they stopped the loss of blood.

The aid unit rushed Marty off to the emergency room.

The investigation of Marty's shooting was moving full speed by the police crime scene units investigating the house and patrol shook down any suspicious person found in the area.

In the meantime, Dick sat by Marty's bedside and waited for her to wake up.

At the end of the second day, and from the lack of sleep, Dick dozed off.

"Wake up, Detective Diamond," a weak voice whispered.

Dick woke and believed he was hearing things and readjusted himself.

Then he heard the voice again. "Detective Diamond."

Dick readjusted himself and opened his eyes to check on Marty.

"Marty, you're awake," Dick whispered.

With a weak voice, Marty said, "I hope so, if I'm not, I'm dead."

"Are you strong enough to talk?"

"I can talk a little, I don't remember much," Marty explained.

"Are you sure you have the strength?"

"Sure, by the way, you look like hell," Marty whispered.

"I'm fine now. What happened back at your home," Dick asked?

In a weak voice, Marty said, "After I left the office, I went straight home and to the kitchen for a glass of wine. When I opened the fridge, a man stepped from the basement door. Out of reflex, I kicked the door, knocking the man back down the stairs, giving me time to call the cops. But before I could call 911, the man came back. I fought him off and was able to run down into the basement, and while I was crawling up the old coal shute to escape, the killer found me, and without saying a word, he shot me. That's all I can remember."

"I wonder what that man was after. Why would he want to kill you for no reason," Dick questioned.

"I could identify him, and that forced him to kill me. Why was he in my house? I don't know. I do know this trouble started with the arrival of Peggy," Marty stated.

"Peggy's case is a lot of trouble, and it's moving fast," Dick said.

"Did you go home after I left the office?" Marty asked.

"No, I went out to eat and then drove out to the address Peggy gave me. I wanted to see if she lived alone. At daybreak, I returned to the office," Dick explained.

"You know, Dick, there may have been a killer at your house waiting for you," Marty suggested.

"That's true, and again, we ask the question, why anyone would want to kill us," Dick said.

"There is a reason. We just don't know why."

"Someone doesn't want us to take Peggy's contract and is willing to kill to prevent us from finding out what's behind Jamie vanishing, or it could be someone sending Peggy a message: if she continues to look for Jamie, she will die," Dick explained.

"Why don't they just kill Peggy," Marty asked?

"Killing Peggy would shine a light on the killer and change the case from a missing person to a homicide. They don't want that for some unknown reason," Dick suggested.

"It's going to be up to you to investigate this case, Detective Diamond, I'm in no condition to help," Marty exclaimed!

"You will be out of here in no time," Dick commented as he stood up to leave.

"Goodbye, Dick, see you tomorrow," Marty whispered as she turned off the bedside lamp.

Dick left the hospital and drove home. He pulled into the driveway, turned off the engine and sat for a time. At this point, he didn't give a damn if there was a killer out there or not. He was too tired.

The next thing Dick knew was that his neighbor Jesse was tapping on the window of his car and asking if he was okay.

"Yes, Jesse, thanks, I'm fine, I was tired when I came home last night and fell asleep while sitting in the car," Dick said.

"By the way, there was a white convertible Cadillac that stopped by your house last night about thirty minutes before you drove up. I watched a man get out of the Cadillac and ring the doorbell. He looked in the windows, then he walked over to the door and did something, then he left," Jesse stated.

"Thank you, Jesse, I'll see if he left a message," Dick said as he got out of the car and looked around as he walked toward the front door.

Dick started to unlock the door when he noticed a card stuck between the door and the door jam. He removed the card and read it. *We are watching you, leave Peggy's case alone or die.* He slipped the card into his pocket, unlocked the door and walked in.

In the living room Dick poured a drink and listened to the morning news before he headed for the shower.

By midmorning, he had showered, shaved, eaten, and started to have another cup of coffee when the phone rang. The phone rang again and again until Dick finally picked it up.

"Hello, Diamond speaking."

"Just listen, I left you a note on the door. Now, I'm watching you right now, and you are a slow-minded fool if you don't heed that message," the voice stated.

"Okay, sir, if I stop, then what," Dick responded.

There was silence on the phone for a few seconds, then the gruff voice with an accent said, "If you want to live without fear of dying, you will walk away from the case. You involved an organization that will smash you like a bug."

By this time, Dick had all he could stand and shouted, "Who in the hell do you think you are telling me what to do, you son of a bitch!"

The phone went dead.

CHAPTER 3

IN THE FOG, WE ARE

Dick remembered his promise to the sheriff's office and the Bellingham Police to report what had been happening to him.

He drove to the sheriff's office, where he found two detectives standing at the front counter as if they were waiting for him.

"Come in and follow us, Mr. Diamond," one of the detectives requested, "there is someone here to meet with you."

Diamond followed them to a meeting room where he was introduced to a Coast Guard Warrant Officer Ned Steven.

Diamond sat across from the coast guard, officer and Peggy.

"Okay, I can see this is not just a friendship meeting, what's going on," Diamond asked with some anger in his voice?

"Well, Mr. Diamond, you are here at the request of Peggy Powers," the coast guard warrant officer stated.

"Okay, I'm here. What's going on," Diamond asked?

"We found Jamie and her friend Bodie White. Their bodies were found just off of Spencer Spit on Lopez Island, tangled to a buoy anchor line in thirty feet of water."

"Who found them, and what happened to them," Dick asked?

"A boater was securing his boat to a buoy when he saw two bodies tangled onto the anchor line ten feet down. At first, the boater thought the bodies were mannequins until he pulled them up with a retrieving pole. When he grabbed the arm of the female, the skin peeled off.

The boater dropped the body back in the water and called the coast guard on his marine radio. The coast guard arrived at the boaters' location and brought the bodies aboard their boat, to the coast guard station and to start the investigation. The bodies had been turned over to the coroner for an autopsy," Warrant Officer Steven explained.

"What kind of evidence was found at the time the bodies were taken from the anchor line," Dick asked?

"Nothing was found at the Spencer Spit location. The investigators believe the two entered the water at another place. We are looking for that place now," the warrant stated.

"Representing Mrs. Powers, what investigation has been taken thus far," Dick asked?

"The sheriff has a team searching the shoreline of Spencer Spit. They believed they found the crime scene at Doe Bay. We will know more later. The CG boats are searching the water for evidence at those two locations. Now we wait to see what the coroner finds," Sheriff Meeks explained.

"Are you sure they were killed at Doe Bay?"

"At this point, we believe they were killed there. That is where the sheriff found a camping sight and her car," Detective Meeks stated.

"There is one item of evidence I think is very important. The two bodies were tied together face to face suggesting a love pact," Warrant Officer Steven explained.

"Okay, I understand what's happening. What can I do? I'm not a law enforcer?" Diamond stated.

"Miss Powers wants you in the investigation because she's not able to keep up with the operations. You are going to be her liaison and maybe help the departments," Meeks stated.

If you don't work for her, she will not file any reports or sign any statements. We need for you to go with us to help," Warrant Officer Steven stated.

"What do you say, Peggy," Diamond questioned?

"Yes. I want you to stay on the case as my representee," Peggy stated.

"Okay, who do I go with to see the bodies at the morgue," Diamond asked?

"You will go with the coast guard. They are in charge of the investigation at this point. When their investigation is completed, then you will be with me, I'm the San Juan County Sheriff's Officer in charge," Detective Paul Meeks explained.

Detective Paul Pitman of the Bellingham Police spoke up, "This is the San Juan Sheriff's Department case, and our department will support the sheriff's office on this case."

"For the rest of the day, let's return to our departments and review the reports and get a fresh start tomorrow. We will meet at this station at nine o'clock tomorrow to exchange information and come up with leads," Detective Meeks stated.

There was a unanimous, "Good, let's go," from the group.

"We'll see you all tomorrow," Detective Meeks responded.

Everybody got up and left the interview room except Peggy and Diamond.

Peggy told Dick she felt there was more to this than a suicide.

"What do you mean, Peggy," Dick asked?

"Jamie wasn't raped or beaten, nor was her friend. The strange thing is why were they tied together. There wasn't any kind of a love affair, Jamie is gay. What does this mean," Peggy asked?

"I don't know, Peggy, I will be at the police station tomorrow morning for you, and I will ask that question," Dick assured Peggy as they walked out of the station.

As Dick drove to the hospital to see Marty he noticed a black BMW following him, then it disappeared two blocks from the hospital.

Dick had a feeling there was a lot more to this case than just killing. He thought those two young people were into something bad. Someone tried to kill Marty because of his investigation. He knew there was big trouble ahead. Unfortunately, the only thing he could do was play the hand given to him in hopes of saving Marty and himself.

Dick pulled into the hospital parking lot and went into the hospital.

In Marty's room, Dick woke her to see how she was doing. He told her about his threats and said to make sure she watched out for anyone coming into her room.

Marty said she was fine and ready to go home and help Dick. She also believed the only way they could be free was to find the killer.

Dick also filled Marty in on Jamie's case and encouraged her to stay in the hospital for her safety until she fully recovered.

Marty was quick to say, "I am getting out tomorrow. I will not stay while you are out working your ass off trying to save our lives."

"I know there's no stopping you, Marty," Dick said as he said good night, see you tomorrow.

"Get the hell out of my room, Detective Diamond," Marty exclaimed with a big smile.

With their goodbyes said, Dick left the hospital and headed home.

At sunup the next morning, Dick had his coffee and then headed for his office before going to the police station to get his unanswered question asked.

As Dick backed out of the driveway he noticed a white Cadillac convertible sitting about a block away. There was a person sitting behind the steering wheel.

The Cadillac followed for two blocks, then it turned away.

Another car is following me. Is this a killer stalking or just another warning, Dick thought as he drove on.

CHAPTER 4

GOING DEEPER INTO THE KILLING

Diamond changed his mind about going to his office; he headed to the police station and pulled into the police parking lot. He looked around for the white Cadillac, but it was nowhere to be seen.

Dick walked into the police station conference room where detectives and Warrant Officer Steven were sitting, having coffee and talking about Jamie's case.

Dick sat down by the coast guard officer when Peggy walked in and sat down by him.

"Good morning, Detective Diamond," Peggy said warmly.

"Good morning, Peggy, why are you here," Diamond asked?

"I couldn't sleep, and I was worried. I needed to see how this operation is going to start out," Peggy said.

"I couldn't sleep either, too many loose ends in this investigation," Diamond explained.

"I hope we can find something out about how they are going to start to investigate," Peggy suggested.

"Lets' see what leads the group has come up with," Diamond stated as he patted the back of Peggy's hand.

Detective Meeks stood up and stated, "We have all read the reports. So what kind of leads have we developed?"

There was an eerie quietness in the room; no one had a lead.

Meeks spoke up, "Does anyone have a suggestion?"

A Bellingham detective spoke up, "My department will work on the backgrounds of Jamie and her associates in Bellingham."

The coast guard warrant officer stated he would background Jamie and her friend Bodie White through the federal side and Interpol.

Detective Meeks agreed and said his department would continue searching out the crime scene and canvas the area where the victims were camping and where their bodies were found.

The Bellingham detective asked, "Diamond, could you canvas the places Jamie visited?"

"Sure, I will work on that as soon as we finish here," Diamond responded.

"I think we have a good start to pick up a lead or two. While all of you are working, I will keep you posted on the coroner's report and compile reports coming in from investigations. We will meet again tomorrow, same time and same place," Meeks stated.

The meeting was over, and everybody left except for Peggy and Diamond.

"Peggy, while we wait for some leads, I'm going to nose around town and Peggy, can you tell me anything more about Jamie or her friends?"

Peggy thought for a minute, then said, "Jamie didn't go out much, she was heavy into computers and classes through the university here in Bellingham. She spent most of her time with Bodie because he was also crazy about computers. As for Bodie, he was a bartender, part-time, just for money to live on. I don't think Bodie had any friends either."

"Thanks, Peggy, I'll start with the taverns in town," Diamond said.

Peggy and Diamond left the station and went their own ways.

Diamond drove uptown to one of the town's oldest restaurants, the Horseshoe Restaurant, where he had lunch.

While having lunch, Diamond asked the waitress if they knew Bodie. One of the waitresses said they knew him, and found him a quiet loner who only came in with Jamie.

After lunch, Diamond spent the rest of the day canvassing the taverns along Railroad Avenue and adjacent streets. He was hoping to find where Bodie had worked.

While Diamond worked the bars, he noticed a black BMW that kept showing up.

It was plain to Dick this person was following him, and it was time to find out who and why he was being followed.

Dick had finished talking with a bartender on Railroad Avenue and looked out a big window of the tavern to see the BMW parked across the street. Dick asked the bartender to let him go through the kitchen and out the back door to catch a thief.

The bartender agreed, and within a couple of minutes, Dick had run out the back door, down the alley, and across the street two cars behind the BMW.

Dick could see a redhead behind the steering wheel starting to leave. Dick rushed up to the driver's door, jerked it open, and pushed over the driver until he was behind the steering wheel.

Dick was surprised to see the redhead was a woman and quickly said, "Where would you like me to drive you, miss?"

"Get out of my car, you bastard," the woman shouted as she reached for her handbag on the floor.

"No, you don't, honey. Your bag is now mine," Dick responded as he grabbed her handbag!

"Who are you," she screamed!

"I'm the man you've been following," Dick said as he pulled a 9mm Sig Sauer gun from her handbag.

What's with the 9mm Sig? Are you afraid someone will kill you?"

The woman said nothing while trying to twist her arm out of Diamond's hand.

"Do you want to talk to me or the police as to why you are stalking me," Diamond asked?

"Why don't we go to the police station. I'll talk to the police," the redhead said.

"Sure," Diamond responded as he pulled the gearshift into drive.

Nothing was said until a block away from the Bellingham Police Station when the woman said, "Turn right at the next light."

Dick reminded her that they would be driving away from the station.

"I know, but I need to tell you something before we talk to the police," the redhead stated.

Dick pulled over to the curb and asked, "Who in the hell are you, and what do you want?"

"I'm not going to tell you just yet. I will tell you something important. Tomorrow the sheriff will tell you that Jamie and Bodie committed a love suicide pact, which is bull. They were killed. I'm telling you this because I may need your help and your trust to get my job done," the redheaded woman explained.

"I'm sure you know I'm a private investigator, and I'm not working on any case you know of. So I ask you what you are after," Diamond said.

"Oh, yes, you are, Private Detective Dickson Diamond. You are working on the Jamie case, and that's the case I'm working on," the redhead stated.

Dick was totally confused about this vague story she told him, and without further ado, Dick said, "I'll take you back to the tavern, and you can go on your way."

Nothing was said again while driving back to the tavern. At the tavern Dick slid out of the car and said goodbye to the redheaded woman.

She said nothing and drove away without looking up.

Dick walked over to the tavern, sat on a stool, ordered a double shot of tequila and slammed one down.

I talked to a woman and didn't learn one thing about her, not even her name, he thought to himself.

"Give me one more shot," Dick told the bartender.

After his third shot, he headed to his car and drove home.

The next day, at the meeting, Detective Meeks stood up and stated, "This case is closed. The coroner has declared the two deaths a suicide, it was a love pact between Jamie and Bodie. Thanks for all the help you and your departments have given my department."

Dick was surprised to hear a suicide love pact declared by the coroner's final report. This is what the curious redheaded woman told him yesterday. How did she know it was going to be classified a suicide?

Peggy looked at Dick and said, "Bullshit, those two were just friends. As I told you earlier, Jamie was gay."

"I'm not finished looking into this killing," Dick responded to Peggy as he got up to leave the station.

Later in the day, Dick was having a beer in the Waterfront Tavern in old town, thinking about the redhead. Suddenly, the redhead came in and sat at the bar beside him.

"What did Detective Meeks say about the deaths," the redhead asked?

"Just what you said yesterday. The coroner classified the death as a suicide. How did you know what the coroner was going to classify the case as?"

"I can't tell you. I can say the coroner is in an awful spot. The coroner had to file a case of suicide to save his wife. For now, we have to leave it at that. Now, if I have gained your trust, can you help me," the redhead questioned?

With anger in his voice, Dick said, "You won't tell me your name or who you work for, and yet you want me to trust you? Don't you think that's a bit much?

The redhead asked the bartender to bring her a brandy.

"Okay, but before I help, you will tell me who you are and who you work for," Dick stated.

"I'll make a deal with you. If you help me, I will help you when I can," the redhead responded.

"That's a tall order, and just how can you help me?"

"I have contacts you don't," the redhead commented.

Before Diamond could say anything, she slid off the barstool and said, "I will contact you later," and walked out.

Dick watched as this tall, long-legged, redhead walked away from him, and for the first time since his wife passed away, Dick found himself interested in another woman and, at the same time, a little guilty, admiring this woman's perfectly balanced body.

She is beautiful, Dick thought as he slipped off the stool, headed to his car and drove home feeling very confused about this encounter.

At home, Dick had two shots of port and went to bed.

After shower and coffee the next morning, Dick headed out pounding the pavement looking for that one good lead that would clue him to Peggy's sweet daughter's killer.

CHAPTER 5

THERE'S A CRACK IN THE CASE

After a hard day pounding the pavement and canvassing where Jamie lived, Dick returned home. When he opened the front door, he noticed someone had slipped an envelope under the door. He picked it up and laid it on the table.

Dick walked over to his overstuffed leather chair and removed his 357 shoulder holster, hanging it on the coat rack nearby. He poured a shot of brandy and sat down.

Before he had his first drink, the phone rang. He picked up and said, "Hi, Marty, what's up?"

"I thought I'd let you know I'm home and ready to work. When can I meet you for an update on Jamie's case?"

"We can meet tomorrow at the Colophon Restaurant in Fairhaven at eleven in the morning. They have a great lunch," Dick explained.

"See you at eleven," Marty responded.

Dick hung up the phone and finished his brandy then he opened the envelope to read the hand written note, "Look into Jamie's computer history and her interest in Chinese studies. I warn you, once you go into her computer, your life will get very dangerous. Burn this after reading."

"That note is from the redhead. What the hell have I gotten myself into?" Dick wondered as he burned the note.

The next morning, Dick went to Peggy's home to gather additional information on Jamie and collect her computer and any emails she may have left lying around.

At Peggy's home on South Hill, Dick was invited in, and after their cordial morning greeting, they sat down in the living room with coffee.

Dick informed Peggy about the threats he had received and Marty being shot. This had all happened after taking her case. The shooting made it clear to him that he was on the right track to finding the killers.

Dick told Peggy about Jamie's computers: he would like to have them before the killers came for them.

Peggy was happy to give up her computers, explained that Jamie took a lot of computer classes at the university and, at times, worked for some government agency. A woman would come and drop off computer work for Jamie.

Dick asked if Jamie talked about the kind of computer work she did for this person.

Peggy explained, "Jamie would only say it was low-level information she put into the computer, but she would not say what kind of information it was or who she worked for."

"What do you know about Bodie? Did he work with Jamie and the government also?"

"I know nothing about Bodie, Jamie only said Bodie didn't have a family, and he was a loner. Outside of that, Jamie said nothing about him," Peggy commented.

Diamond thanked Peggy and took the computer and cell phone to the sheriff's department to turn over to Meeks.

As Diamond started to enter the main door of the police station to get an update on the Bellingham Police report on Jamie's case, he caught a glimpse of the redheaded woman as she drove off.

Knowing he couldn't catch up with her, he continued on into the station.

For some reason, Diamond was told by the desk officer, the case was closed as a suicide, and the files were sent to the archives. Dick realized the Bellingham Police were not going to get involved with a private detective. He thanked the officer and left the station.

Dick called Marty to tell her the case was closed at the Bellingham Department, and now he was going to the sheriff's office to see if Meeks could help. He would call Marty back as soon as he could.

"No problem, I've got a lot to do on other cases, I'll see you when I see you coming through the door," Marty responded.

"Thanks, Marty, I'll call you."

Instead of going to the sheriff's office, Dick drove to Peggy's home to tell her what had happened at the Bellingham Police Station, and that the case was closed.

At Peggy's, Dick asked if she wanted to continue investigating, and he said, "Before you answer, I may get some help from the San Juan County Sheriff's Office and the U.S. Coast Guard."

Peggy asked Dick what he thought about the law enforcement agencies.

Dick explained that there were some unanswered questions, and he would work to answer them even if the Bellingham Police closed the case.

Suddenly there was an interrupting knock on the front door.

"Who could that be? My only friend is out of town," Peggy responded as she walked over to the door.

Peggy opened the door, and there stood a tall, redheaded woman.

"May I help you, miss," Peggy asked.

"May I come in? I have something to tell you about Jamie."

"Yes! Please come in," Peggy suggested.

The redhead walked over to where Dick was seated and sat in a chair by him.

Peggy sat across from them.

"Miss Powers, I'm here investigating the case of Jamie and Bodie. I must tell you some things to get answers from you," the redhead said.

"I understand, miss, but first, who are you," Peggy asked?

"I'm also interested in hearing the answers," Dick interrupted.

"I work for the FBI, and my name is Agent Susan Tomas. I have come from Washington, DC, to find out what happened to Jamie and Bodie. She worked as a computer entry data operator for NSA. Now, that's all I can say."

"Are you not working with local police," Peggy asked?

"The local police cannot help me. They saw this case as a local love suicide and closed the case. NSA believed Jamie or Bodie had found out about some kind of a Chinese operation in Puget Sound and asked the FBI to look into it. NSA believed Jamie had hacked into the Chinese army computer system, and the Military Red Army found out about Jamie's hacking and had to stop her. This is only a speculation by the FBI at this time," Agent Susan Tomas said.

"My god, this is a federal case, that's why the Bellingham Police closed the case."

"That's right, Dick, and this information must stay within the three of us," Susan stated.

"I can go along with you for now," Dick stated.

"Dick, we must work together without alerting the police or anyone else until I'm ready to inform them," Susan explained.

"I can work with you, Susan, because I need the truth about what happened to Jamie for my peace of mind," Peggy clarified.

Diamond spoke up, "Peggy wants me to stay on the case, and that means we will work together to solve this case."

"We will share our information," Susan stated.

"Sure, but I don't know anything," Peggy said as she poured a glass of sherry.

"Susan, you have told us little about Jamie," Dick said.

"I don't know much, my orders stated that Jamie was a low-level programmer for the NSA computer systems. As I have said, NSA believes Jamie stumbled onto a deep Chinese undercover group working in this area when Jamie was killed. That is all the FBI knows," Susan explained.

"Where do we go from here," Peggy asked?

"I'm going back to the streets and work the people who may have some information about Bodie and work from that angle to find a lead," Diamond explained.

"I'll go back to the FBI labs and recheck the evidence. There may be something we've missed," Susan said as she got up to leave.

"I'll stay home and wait for someone to call and tell me what happened to my sweet girl," Peggy stated.

With the conversation over, Susan and Dick left Peggy's home.

Outside Peggy's home, Dick told Susan he felt better now that he knew who this redhead was.

Susan smiled and said, "We will solve this case together."

At that point, Susan headed to the Bellwether Hotel where she was staying.

Diamond stopped at one of his watering holes, the Boundary Bay Brewery, for a cool beer before hitting the hot street.

As he drank his beer and pondered over what Susan had said, a beautiful Chinese woman came in, sat down by him, and said, "Hi, Dick."

Diamond was taken aback by this beautiful woman and responded by offering her a drink before thinking.

"Don't get excited, Dick, I stopped on my way to Vancouver to tell you to stop your investigation. Your nosing into the Jamie case will get you killed," the Asian woman explained.

Diamond was stunned and said nothing; he just sat and watched the lady leave.

What the hell was that all about, Dick thought?

Dick left the bar, headed for the door, and started his canvassing on the street for information about Bodie.

For the rest of the day Dick walked and talked to anyone around the Skylark Restaurant and Bar, and without any luck, he stopped and headed home to rest his tired feet.

The next morning, Dick called that special number Susan gave him and left her a message to meet him at noon in Boulevard Park; he had something to tell her.

At noon sharp, Susan pulled into Boulevard Park and parked by Diamond's car. The two walked into Woods Coffee Shop and sat by a big window looking out over the bay. While they had coffee, Dick told Susan about the Chinese woman.

Susan didn't hesitate to say, "Dick, I know the woman, she works for DEA. She's been told to find you and stop you from investigating Jamie. This means the DEA must be working on a drug case involving Bodie."

"I don't give a damn about the DEA. I'm concerned about Peggy and who killed Jamie," Dick explained.

"I know, Dick, I will talk to my boss about the DEA," Susan explained.

"Have you gained information from the lab," Diamond asked?

"No, the coast guard turned over some additional evidence to the lab. As soon as I hear something, I'll let you know. What is your next move, Dick," Susan asked?

"I'm going to the coast guard station and talk to the warrant officer about the deaths. What about you, Susan?"

While I wait for the lab results, I'll go to the university and see what I can find out at the school's Chinese department. I may find some information about some Chinese operation Jamie found. I should be back later tonight," Susan said.

As Susan pulled out of the parking lot, Dick noticed a black SUV that pulled out and followed her at a distance.

Dick called Susan on her phone, "Susan, you have a black SUV following you. Watch yourself," Diamond stated, stressfully.

"I know, I've been watching. I think it's DEA, but not sure," Susan explained.

"I can follow you and the SUV as your backup," Diamond stated.

"No, let me deal with this, I'll call you later," Susan responded.

Dick agreed and said, "I'll see you when I see you."

CHAPTER 6

JAMIE'S DEATH CONFIRMED

At the coast guard station, Diamond was admitted and met with the warrant officer in charge, Ned Steven.

"Good morning, Officer Steven. I stopped by to see if you had found any additional evidence on Jamie," Diamond asked?

"I'm glad you stopped by, I do have a couple of items of interest. Let me show you."

Officer Steven laid out a group of pictures taken on the day Jamie was found. "These two bodies tied together are Jamie and Bodie. Look at the way they were tied together. These are not nautical knots—they are used by special trained people like agents or equestrians."

"What are you saying," Dick asked?

"I'll tell you, Jamie and Bodie were tied up by someone that uses these kinds of knots. Secondly, they didn't have any water in their lungs and they were dead before their bodies hit the water. I rechecked the bodies via a coast guard contract coroner. He found a small-caliber hole in the back of their heads just behind the right ear. The other coroner overlooked these holes. The autopsy showed these bullet holes were made by a .22 caliber at a close range, maybe one inch," Steven concluded.

"This means the first report was prejudged before a complete autopsy was made, for some reason. That needs to be looked into," Dick stated.

"I believe so. I haven't talked to the police since they closed the case as a suicide," Steven said.

"Could we hold up showing these crime scene pictures for a day or so," Dick suggested.

"Sure, the police have closed the case, and they will need evidence to reopen it," Officer Steven replied with a smile.

Dick thanked Officer Steven, left the station, and headed to Bodie's studio room by Dirty Harry's Steak House. He needed to recheck for any missed clues.

At Bodie's studio room Dick noticed an Asian man leaving with a clean-up cart. *This is odd, cleaning up a room weeks after Bodie's death,* Dick pondered.

"What are you doing in the room," Dick asked?

"I'm the clean-up person, I just finished cleaning the room so the room can be rented out," the Asian man said as he walked down the hallway away from Dick.

With the room cleaned, Dick found nothing and left. As he walked by the office that rented out the rooms, he stopped and asked the young lady behind the desk, "Who gave the cleaning man the okay to clean Bodie's room?"

The lady looked up from her book and asked, "What would you like to know about the cleaning of the rooms?"

"I'm a private investigator, and I just talked to a cleaning man who just cleaned room no. 3. That room was rented to Bodie White, who was killed weeks ago," Dick stated.

"Sir, we don't have a clean-up man. The renters clean their own room at the end of their contract, and I clean the room just before renting the room out to a new person. I don't know who that clean-up man was," the lady responded.

Dick thanked her and left, knowing he had just been screwed by a possible Chinese agent, but that wasn't all bad because now, he had a lead.

Dick spent the rest of the day canvassing the area for information about that Chinese man.

By sundown, Dick had found one woman who had observed Bodie talking to an Asian man and woman. They were in a white convertible Cadillac outside of Dirty Dans. She noticed Bodie because of that sharp classic Cadillac.

Dick finished his canvassing and headed home. As he pulled up in front of his house, he saw Susan sitting on his porch steps. He walked up to her and asked, "Aren't you taking a chance sitting out in the open on my porch?"

"No," Susan stated as she reached out her hand for Dick to help her stand up. And she adjusted her black skirt, saying, "The killer knows I'm after him. Thanks for helping me up."

"Okay, your cover is blown, do you want to come in for a drink."

"Why not? I need a drink after that long trip to Seattle and back," Susan said with a smile.

Susan and Dick walked into the house, knowing they were probably being watched.

Once in the living room, Dick pulled the drapes and poured Susan and himself a shot of brandy. He handed it to her as he said, "Salute."

Susan held up her glass and responded, "Salute!"

"Tell me what you found out about our killer," Dick asked?

Susan explained that she talked to and showed Bodie's picture to a lot of people working in the office and students in Chinese studies.

A couple of students saw Bodie and a Chinese man at the student union having coffee. They didn't believe Bodie was a student and he had no reason to be at the university. They thought the Asian man was a professor.

Dick butted in, "Speaking of Chinese, I found a Chinese man snooping around Bodie's apartment, but I didn't get any information out of him."

"We have a couple of leads directing us to the Chinese. This is something we can work on while we wait for the lab results," Susan responded.

"Yes, we do!"

"Our investigating is directing us toward the Chinese. This could be an international situation," Susan stated.

"Yes, it looks that way. This all started with Jamie hacking into the Chinese Army computers," Dick commented.

"But we must not forget Bodie, who was very close to Jamie. Remember, NSA found him talking via telephone to someone in Mexico."

"That phone call to Mexico may have connected him with cartels, and that's why the DEA is involved, does this mean Bodie is involved with drugs," Dick asked?

"I did find one more point of interest that will support the Chinese theory. A student told me she saw Bodie talking to a man about two blocks away from the university, a known drug area. This man was Chinese," Susan said.

"What the hell was Bodie doing in the university district two times that we know of," Dick asked?

"I don't know, but we may be in the middle of an international drug incident," Susan said with concern in her voice.

"If you are right, what have the Chinese got to do with drugs? We must watch each other's back to stay alive," Dick stressed.

"Yes, and as soon as I have a little more proof, I will report the operations to the DEA and let them have the case," Susan commented.

Looking at her watch, Susan said, "It's getting late. I'd better get back to the hotel."

"Why don't you stay the night? I have a guest room, and we can order Panda for dinner. This way, you can be safe, we can try to figure out our next investigation directions and you won't be taking a risk driving across town," Dick stated.

"Sure, I can stay, but you sleep in your room, and I will sleep in the guest room, is that something you can agree on?"

"Susan, I don't want to sleep with you. I would never sleep with a working partner," Dick responded.

"Good, now order the Panda, I'm starving," Susan demanded.

Susan and Dick ate and worked to find a path to the Chinese operations or Mexican drugs.

Susan was working on finding the killer of Jamie and Bodie. She said the FBI found Bodie had a relationship with a Chinese student at the university and the CIA found out this student was a woman in the Red Army. She may be working with others at the university," Susan added.

With this information, Dick could see why the local Police were not involved; this was a national problem. He also realized the only way they could save their asses was to find a clear path to drugs or a Chinese operation before they could solve the case.

The night ended with Susan in the guest room and Dick in his room, both having a good night's sleep. The next morning, at 6:00 a.m., Dick was up having coffee when Susan came out of the guest room in one of Dick's robes.

"Morning, Dick," Susan said as she passed him, heading to the shower.

Dick handed her a cup of coffee and asked, "Are you going to the university today?"

"Yes. I'm working on the possibility this is a spy operation," Susan said.

By eight o'clock, the two were out of the house, heading for their prospective investigations.

Susan headed to the university in Seattle to find this woman who was a friend of Bodie.

Dick would search for the Chinese man who outsmarted him yesterday at Bodie's apartment.

At the university, Susan found a Chinese woman that knew Bodie. This student said there was a woman by the name of Chung Me Li, a guest speaker who was introduced to Bodie. The student said she had seen Bodie with Chung Me Li only once.

Susan's day was over, and she headed back to Bellingham.

As for Dick, he found nothing except a uniform store that rented an Asian man a service uniform. But the store believed the name given on the rental slip was bogus. The name was Mr. Jim Jones. The day was over, and Dick headed home.

By the time Susan had arrived back in Bellingham she was too tired to find a place to eat and called Dick to meet him at Dirty Dan's in Fairhaven for a great steak.

Dick agreed, left the house, and met Susan. Soon the two were eating and discussing their gains of the day.

After dinner, Susan and Dick were having coffee when Dick suddenly leaned over and lightly kissed Susan.

"There is a Chinese man watching us," Dick whispered.

Understanding what Dick was telling her, Susan followed through and slowly kissed Dick back.

She whispered, "I'm only kissing you to make this man think we're lovers."

Dick smiled and said, "That's fine, I enjoyed the kiss anyway. You know this kiss means you will have to stay at my place tonight to convince that man we are truly lovers. He will follow us when we leave," Dick whispered.

"As long as I can sleep in the guest room," Susan said with a smile.

The two finished their coffee and headed out of the restaurant for Dick's home and to see if that Chinese man followed.

The Chinese man did follow for a short distance and turned off toward the Bay.

By the time they had settled down in the living room at Dick with a brandy, Susan said, "I'm ready for bed."

"Sure, me too," Dick clarified.

Early the next morning, Dick was having coffee when Marty came in the back door leading into the kitchen as she always did.

"Good morning, Dick, how's the leads opening up on our case?"

At that moment, Susan came into the kitchen, surprising Marty.

"Good morning," Marty surprisingly stated.

"Marty, this is Agent Susan Tomas of the FBI. She will be working with us on the case. Susan, this is Martha Mills, my partner in the investigation business. We all call her Marty."

"Good morning, Marty," Susan responded coolly because of the new face.

Susan felt a little easier after the three had their coffee and talked about Dick and Marty's agency.

Marty then informed Dick and Susan she tricked a male bartender into talking about Bodie, who she had seen in the bar before. He told her he had seen an Asian woman with Bodie in a parking lot near the bar a week or so before Bodie went missing.

"Good work, Marty, when can we talk to him?"

"Anytime, but I have to call him to get time to meet," Marty said.

"How do you feel about Marty working with us, Susan," Dick questioned?

"She's your partner, and I'm fine with that," Susan stated.

"Marty, you and Susan need to get to know one another, so, Susan, is it okay if the two of you meet with the bartender to interview him?"

"Yes, that's fine," Susan responded.

"I don't have a problem with that," Marty acknowledged.

"In the meantime, I'll continue searching for that Asian cleaning man who outsmarted me. I'll stop by and see Meeks to update him on what we have so far. We can meet at six at Dirty Dan's to compare notes," Dick suggested.

After the two women left, Dick headed out in search of that Cadillac that Bodie and the Asian woman were seen in.

CHAPTER 7

———

THE SEARCH

At six o'clock at night, Marty and Susan walked into Dirty Dan's Steak House, expecting to see Dick having a drink at a table, but he wasn't there.

"Lets' have a drink while we wait for Dick," Marty suggested.

By 6:30, Dick hadn't arrived, and he didn't answer his phone when Marty tried to call him.

"We have a problem. Something has happened to Dick," Marty said.

"Yes, I think you're right. I'll call the police, hospital, and tow companies while you drive around looking for his car," Susan said as the two walked out to their cars.

"When I call the police I will tell them who I am in hopes of getting extra help. This means the police will learn who I am, but it can't be helped," Susan explained.

"Susan, I'll go back to Skylark and ask for the bartender's help," Marty stated.

At the Skylark, Marty met with the bartender, but he couldn't help; all he could tell her was that the Asian woman's Cadillac stayed in the Fairhaven boatyard most of the time. That car may have something to do with the case.

Marty thanked the bartender and left, looking for the Caddy and Dick.

As she searched for a short time, Marty found Dick's car partly hidden behind an empty building in the Fairhaven boatyard. Then she called Susan for backup.

Susan arrived shortly, pulled in behind Marty's car and got out to back Marty.

Susan said she called the police and that they would come as soon as they could; they were dealing with a fight with knives at the Waterfront Tavern.

The two women started toward the side door of the empty building with their weapons out. Susan's eyes searched the second floor of the building for signs of a shooter as Marty searched the area around them. Just before opening the side door, Susan pointed to a second-floor window with a dim light.

"That's where Dick is, and that's where we are going," Marty whispered.

"Yes, stay close to watch each other's backs," Susan quietly responded as she opened the door.

Entering the building, they found empty open space with a staircase leading up to the second floor. Susan pointed to the staircase. Their eyes searched overhead as they walked to it.

They started up the creaky staircase slowly until they were at the top of the stairs.

Just as they started to feel they were getting close to rescuing Dick, a muzzle flashed, and a loud blast roared from a dark area in a hallway.

Immediately, the women hit the floor and fired back in the direction of the muzzle flash. All went quiet.

The silence was broken by someone running down the dark hallway and out the second-floor door.

The two women laid still and were ready to continue firing.

The stillness gave Susan a feeling that they could move but suddenly, she heard a thumping sound coming from the dim-lit room. She motioned to Marty to move forward.

Marty moved ahead of Susan only to stumble over a body lying on the floor. "I found the shooter," she whispered as she checked the body for signs of life. "This is a very dead man."

The two continued on to the open door of the lit room.

Susan peeked around the door jamb for shooters inside. Marty was on her knees to shoot low.

The room looked clear, and they both stepped inside with their guns swinging toward dark areas.

Susan pointed to a tied-up body in the corner of the room.

Marty focused on the body and said, "It's Dick!"

She hurried over to check on his condition and kneeling down she jerked the duct tape from Dick's mouth.

"Dick! Are you okay," she questioned in a panic?

"Son of a bitch, Marty! I think you ripped my lips off! And yes, I'm fine, just my ego is beaten up," Dick responded.

"What the hell happened to you?"

"Hell, I don't know, I was on my way to the Dirty Dan Steak House when I got a call on the cell phone. The caller wanted me to meet a Chinese man at the boatyard in Fairhaven ASAP! He wanted to discuss the death of Bodie. I had to make that contact," Dick explained.

"Why didn't you call me or Susan to let us know where you were and what you were doing?"

"At the time of the call, I was driving by the boatyard gate. I thought this was going to be just a short meeting and didn't think I would need you," Dick explained.

I was there and quickly pulled in and parked by the building.

"Did you make contact with the man we just killed," Susan asked?

"Yes, I did, but I didn't ask one question because someone hit me on the head, knocking me out. When I woke up, I was tied up."

"How many people were there," Susan asked?

"There were two Asian men that I could see. I recognized one as being the cleaning man at Bodie's apartment. I didn't get a good look at the other man," Dick responded.

"What did they want with you, and why didn't they kill you when they started shooting at us," Susan questioned?

"That's the funny thing, why they didn't kill me? I don't know. And they asked me why I was investigating Bodie. They asked me questions that didn't have anything to do with drugs. They seemed confused about the investigation," Dick explained.

"What do you mean they were not interested in drugs," Susan asked?

"I told them we were investigating Bodie for drugs. They said they didn't care about drugs," Dick explained. "But just as it got interesting, they heard you ladies coming up the stairs, stopped talking and took up a position to shoot it out."

"This puts us back to square one, if they aren't moving drugs, then what," Marty stated.

"No, not quite; When the two of you came in the building, that stopped them from questioning me. They are still interested in what we know. They will continue to come after us until they find out what we are after," Dick explained.

"We need to find a way to force them into revealing what they are really after," Susan said.

"I hear the cops coming, we need to go outside to meet them to stay safe," Dick suggested.

Outside the building, the three investigators stood with their hands up.

Soon Dick and the two women were informing the patrol officers what had happened, and that there was a dead man on the second floor. Suddenly, Detective Meeks pulled up.

"Good to see you, Detective Meeks," Dick said.

"What happened?"

After explaining what had happened to Meeks, Dick asked, "Can we three go home and come to the station to fill out a written report tomorrow?"

"Sure, I'll see the three of you in the morning," Meeks said.

Dick and the two women left the crime scene and headed home to rest after that nerve-racking day.

Early the next morning Dick received a phone call from Officer Ned Steven at the coast guard station. He asked Dick for a meeting before Dick went to the sheriff's office; he had something to show him.

Dick agreed to meet at 8 a.m.

At the coast guard station Dick and Warrant Officer Steven sat down and Officer Steven showed Dick some pictures.

"What am I looking at," Dick asked?

Warrant Officer Steven explained the pictures were taken with a night scope camera on the night Jamie and Bodie were killed.

"Why are these pictures just showing up now?" Dick asked.

"They were placed in the nightly report in the boat operations folder and filed. They were just nightly boat reports in the coxswain's patrol report," Steven responded.

"Again, what are we looking at," Dick asked?

"On the night of the killing, one of my boats was out on patrol for drugs coming out of Canada when the engineer on the boat took these pictures. As you can see, the first picture was taken at 2 a.m., and it shows a forty-two-foot boat pulling anchor and getting underway from Doe Bay, where Jamie and Bodie were camping. The patrol boat followed this boat believing there were drugs on board. The crew believed when the boats went through Peavine Pass, drugs or bodies could be dumped. The current would float the bodies to Spencer Spit. The boats headed west to Friday Harbor. This next picture shows the forty-two-foot boat securing up at Friday Harbor."

"What does this boat have to do with the killing," Dick asked?

"After the suspect boat was secure, our boat crew boarded the boat searching for drugs and found none. All they found were two men who said they were just out cruising. Here is the picture of the two men," Steven explained.

As Dick looked over the pictures, he asked Officer Steven what he thought was going on with these two men.

"This boat was at the place and time of the deaths. Getting underway this time of morning is unusual and dangerous; leaving from Doe Bay by this size boat," Steven replied.

"I think these two men may be able to tell you something about the killings. They could be the killers and could have dumped the bodies off the boat when clearing Peavine Pass," Steven said.

"That makes sense, but the drug operation isn't any part of this boat. The crew didn't find drugs on the boat," Dick said.

"Maybe they were killed for another reason by someone else. We need to talk to these two men to see what they can tell us," Steven replied.

"Can I take these pictures with me?"

"Sure, and when you find out what really happened, let me know," Steven commented.

"By the way, the coast guard will continue their investigations for now, and I'll continue to help you," Steven assured Dick.

"Thanks, I'll keep you posted," Dick responded as he got up to leave.

At the sheriff's office, Dick met with Susan and Marty. They were waiting in the parking lot, and he showed them the pictures.

Marty checked out the pictures closely and commented, "I've seen one man in this picture. He was at the bar when I was talking to bartender Bass. He was sitting at the other end talking to someone on his cell phone."

Marty handed the pictures back to Dick.

"We need to talk about this picture and that man you saw after our meeting with Meeks," Dick stated.

"Sure," Marty said as the three walked into the station for their meeting with Meeks.

In the office, Detective Meeks thanked them for coming in to make their written statements, and said he needed to talk to Susan as to why the FBI was here in Bellingham.

Meeks also informed them that his department would continue investigating Jamie's case because of last night's killing of the Chinese man in the warehouse. He believed the killing was tied to Jamie's killing.

"But, Detective Meeks, the killing of the Chinese man was in the city's jurisdiction, Jamie's was not," Dick explained.

"That's right, Dick, but the Bellingham chief agreed to let the sheriff's department have the case due to that killing, and Jaimie's killing is likely tied with it due to the Chinese being involved," Meeks stated.

The investigators did their reports, and Agent Susan Tomas informed Meeks as to why she was in Bellingham.

By the end of the morning, Meeks had been filled in and the investigators left the Sheriff's office.

In the parking lot, Marty asked, "Why didn't you give Meeks the pictures?"

"I will give them to Meeks later, but first, I want to interview that bartender, Bass, and I don't want to overwhelm him with detectives. He may be one of the people in the picture," Dick replied.

"Marty, why don't the three of us have lunch at the Skylark where Bass works to put him on edge before we interview him? This may encourage him to talk," Dick stated.

Susan didn't stay for lunch or the interview with Bass and headed back to Seattle to gather some information from the immigration office and show the pictures of the dead Chinese man to the school of Chinese studies. She needed to ID him.

CHAPTER 8

THE INTERVIEW

Dick and Marty finished their meal at the bar and noticed Bass had just come to work and seemed to ignore them while he prepared his cash register for his work.

As Bass worked, Dick noticed he was very nervous and asked him, "Is everything okay, Bass?"

Bass looked at Dick and said, "Sure, I just had a hard night working last night."

"Bass! Could you stop for just a minute and look at this picture and tell me who these two people are," Dick stated.

"Okay, let me see the picture," Bass said as he turned from the register.

Bass took the picture with a shaking hand and questioned, "Why do you want to know who these men are?"

"I'm going to be upfront with you, Bass. These men could be part of a murder, and we have to find them for the police. So, Bass, think hard before you answer, you don't want to be part of the death of two people," Dick suggested.

Bass looked at the picture and said, "I don't know these guys."

Bass realized there were cameras in the area and changed his statement, "Wait, I have seen this one man on the right. He has come to the bar for drinks. I have seen him with my friend Bodie. I think Bodie called him Tweed," Bass explained.

"What about the other man?"

"The other guy, I've never seen him before," Bass confirmed.

"Have you seen Tweed with an Asian woman," Marty asked?

"Not in this bar, I did see him with a woman in a convertible Cadillac at a red light in Blaine. I was having lunch with a friend when this caddy stopped at the light," Bass explained.

"Did you get a good look at the two in the car," Dick asked?

"I'm not sure. I think the woman looked Asian, and yes, I'm sure the man was Tweed," Bass acknowledged.

Dick thanked Bass, slipped the picture back into his jacket pocket and told Bass they would see him later.

Dick and Marty left and headed to the boatyard in hopes of finding the Cadillac.

While Dick drove slowly through the boatyard, Marty said, "Maybe Bass is a friend of Bodie and Tweed, and these three could be selling drugs.

Suddenly Marty shouted, "Look over there, isn't that the convertible Cadillac Bass was talking about?"

"Yes, it is, let's see if we can find the owner," Dick stated.

Dick and Marty were looking over the Cadillac when a man came off a boat, cradled high and dry, by the warehouse.

"What are you doing looking at my car," the man asked as he walked up to them?

"Are you the owner of this car?" Dick asked.

"Yes, and what's it to you?" the man asked.

"This car may have been involved in a killing. That's why we are interested in your car. You say you are the owner, which means we need to know your name," Dick stated with some force in his voice.

"If this car is involved in a killing, then my name is none of your business. Who in the hell are you two anyway?"

"We are private investigators working for Mrs. Peggy Powers and the sheriff's department. My name is Dickson Diamond, and this is Martha Mills, my partner. Now, again, what is your name," Dick demanded.

"Well, in that case, my name is Clinton Biltmore. Now, what the hell is the deal with this car," Clinton inquired.

"Your car was seen driven by an Asian woman in Blaine with a man identified by the coast guard on the boat you are working on. That boat was seen in the area the night two people were killed at Doe Bay," Dick advised Clinton.

Clinton quickly responded, "My friend is the owner of the boat I'm working on now."

"Who is this man, and is he in the warehouse now," questioned Dick?

"No, the warehouse is empty. The owner comes down when he wants to use his boat," Clinton advised.

"How do you contact him if you have a question about the boat when you are working on it?"

"I have a phone number for emergency only," Clinton advised.

"This is an emergency. Give me the number," Dick directed.

Clinton reluctantly said he could not give Dick the number, but he would call his friend for Dick.

"Call him."

Clinton pulled out his phone and made the call.

As the phone rang Dick asked, "What is your friend's name?"

The phone stopped ringing, and a voice came on, "Hello."

Clinton said to the person on the phone, "A private detective needs to talk to you about a killing."

Clinton handed Dick the phone and said, "Chung Lee Yu will talk to you."

Dick took the phone, introduced himself and stated he needed to talk to Chung face to face.

Chung agreed and said he would meet Diamond in an hour at the parking lot by the ferry terminal.

Dick agreed and handed the phone back to Clinton.

Dick asked Clinton how long he had known Chung.

"I've known Chung for two years or so," Clinton explained.

"Is Chung married," Dick asked?

"Yes, and I've met her a few times, but I really don't know her. Chung married her when he went back to China visiting his family."

At this point, Dick felt he had enough information from Clinton and thanked him as he and Marty returned to the car.

They left the yard for coffee at Boulevard Park and waited for the meeting with Chung.

One hour passed. They finished their coffee and drove to the ferry terminal.

As they drove into the ferry parking lot, Marty spotted a white convertible Cadillac. "There's Clinton parked over there with someone," Marty directed.

Dick pulled up next to the Cadillac and saw Clinton sitting with another man.

Dick got out of the car, walked over to the passenger's window and asked if the man was Chung.

Chung replied, "Yes."

"Let's go over by the handrail to the terminal and talk," Dick suggested.

The three walked over to the ferry terminal, high over the water, where Dick introduced himself and Marty to Chung.

"What's this all about," Chung Lee Yu asked?

"Well, Mr. Chung, There's a question about this car and your wife driving it. She was seen driving that Cadillac in Blaine with a passenger named Tweed.

On the night Jamie and Bodie went missing, the coast guard took a picture of Tweed on your boat at the scene of a killing," Dick advised.

"I have this picture, please look at it," Dick asked as he handed Chung the picture.

"Thank you, but I know nothing about any of this," Chung responded with surprise.

"Will you help us and the police get the answers to these questions of Jamie," Dick asked?

"Sure, but what does my wife have to do with this killing," Chung asked?

"First, we have to see what she knows about the two people killed. Second, we have to have her tell us about the man in the picture; is he the same as the person seen in Blaine. This man may be the key to the killings. And lastly, what does she know about the man killed last night in your warehouse," Dick explained.

"Come to my home tonight at nine on Chuckanut Drive, and we will try to get to the bottom of this mess," Chung stated.

"We'll see you tonight," Dick said as they returned to their cars.

Later in the day, Dick and Marty met up with Susan at Dick's home, where Susan explained what she had found in Seattle about the Chinese they killed in the warehouse last night.

Susan said, "I met with the head of the Chinese Department at Univ. of WA. and showed him the picture of the dead man. He looked over the picture closely and said he had never seen the man before. He then showed the picture to his assistant and others in the office. They all said they didn't know this man."

"Did the Office of Immigration know this man?" Dick asked.

"They said there was no paper on this man and they had no idea where he came from or who he was," Susan explained.

"Hopefully, we can find out something tonight when we meet with Mrs. Chung," Dick commented.

"Dick, I have to call the office and report what I have found out so far," Susan explained.

"Sure, use the phone in the kitchen."

In the meantime, Marty and Dick discussed what kind of leads they had come up with.

Soon Susan came from the kitchen and told them her boss wanted her to stay on the case. The CIA believes the Chinese are setting up an information-gathering location in the area. That's the word the CIA is getting from Chinese operatives.

Dick and the two ladies left and drove to Fairhaven for a quick dinner before they headed to Mr. Chung's home, where they were hoping to learn who killed Jamie and her friend Bodie.

At nine, they drove up to Mr. Chung's security gate and found it standing open. There was no answer on the gate intercom. "We have a problem," Dick said.

An inspection of the security gate found the lock pried open and Susan said, "Yes, we do have a problem."

"We will leave the car here and walk to the house. Stay in the shadows to make it hard for someone to see us," Dick directed.

The three moved along the shadows until they were at the front door of the house, where Dick found the door ajar and the house lights on.

"Marty, call the police on your cell. Susan and I will see if anyone needs help," Dick said.

Dick slowly pushed open the front door as he pointed his revolver in the direction he was looking. There seemed to be no problem in the room; nothing was disturbed. The two walked together through the first floor of the house and found the rooms clear.

On the second floor, Susan pushed open the bathroom door, and her eyes quickly focused on a body slumped partly over the huge bathtub.

"Dick! Come in here when you finish, I've found a body," Susan shouted as she checked the body for life.

Dick walked into the bathroom to see Susan standing up from the body, "Is the man dead?"

"Yes, he's been dead for a short time, the body isn't cold," Susan slowly responded.

"I hear the police coming. Let's go meet them."

While the three stood out in front of the house, waiting for the police to arrive, Dick told Marty what Susan found upstairs.

Soon Detective Meeks and two patrol units filled up the horseshoe driveway in front of Chung's home; blue and red lights filled the night sky while uniformed officers surrounded the house with their flashlights flashing everywhere.

CHAPTER 9

WHERE DO WE GO NOW?

After the police sealed off the house for the crime lab to investigate, Detective Meeks walked up to the three investigators and said, "Okay, Dick, what's going on this time. You can't stay away from dead people?"

"I know it's late, and I know you were in a warm bed, but because of us, you have an early start on this killing," Dick commented with a big smile.

"Yaa, smartass, now tell me what you know about the dead man, and again, why are you here?"

"We were to meet this dead man's wife and question her about her involvement with a young man named Tweed. She was seen with him, and he may be involved in Jamie's killing," Dick replied.

"What the hell are you talking about? You were to interview a woman here who is connected to the Jamie and Bodie case!" Meeks stated.

"Yes!" Susan said as she butted in, "Don't blame Dick. He was going on my directions."

"And just who in the hell are you," Meeks asked?

"I'm Agent Susan Tomas with the FBI. Remember, we talked before about my investigation?"

"Well, Susan, tell me again, why are you so interested in this investigation," Meeks responded.

"Bodie came to the FBI's attention months ago when he was detected by NSA having a phone conversation with a Chinese person in Mexico. I will stop by your office tomorrow and fill you in on Bodie, Detective Meeks," Susan explained.

"Sure, that's fine," Meeks acknowledged.

For the rest of the night police detectives investigated the crime scene while the coroner prepared to take Chung's body.

Dick informed Meeks about the information he had gathered from the coast guard and Bass. Then he asked Meeks to let the three of them leave and they would stop by and fill out a full report at the sheriff's department tomorrow.

Meeks agreed, said goodnight and would see them tomorrow.

By then, the sun was starting to push back the darkness of the night and Dick asked his partners if they would like to have coffee to clear their heads on what had happened.

The two ladies agreed this would be good, and they all drove to a morning bakery nearby for coffee and éclairs.

Dick sipped his coffee and asked, "Ladies, what leads do we have?"

"Chung's wife may be the key to her husband's death. She is the first on our list," Susan said.

"If there is too much pressure, Chung Me Li may run back to China through Canada," Dick suggested.

"Is that Chung's wife's name," Susan asked?

"Chung told me his wife's name was Chung Me Li," Dick responded.

"I talked to a student at the UW who said there was a guest lector about two years ago by the same name as Chung. This person could be that lector."

"Could be, she may have been here to recon the area for drug sells in the Puget Sound. This area has universities and military everywhere," Dick suggested.

"We need to go back to Bass and find out where Tweed was seen with Chung Me Li in Blaine. I don't think Bass has told us all he knows about Tweed and Chung Me Li," Susan said.

"The bar isn't open now. Let's go home and rest up until ten o'clock. We will meet at the Skylark and interview Bass there," Dick suggested.

"Great," Marty said as the three left the table for their cars.

At ten o'clock, Dick walked into the Skylark restaurant and tavern and saw Susan and Marty sitting at the bar having coffee.

"Hi, ladies, have you seen Bass," Dick commented.

"Yes, he's working at the other end of the bar."

Bass noticed Dick, walked over and asked Dick what would he like to have to drink as he wiped off the counter with a bar towel.

"Give me a cup of coffee, and we have something to talk over with you," Dick stated.

Bass motioned for a waitress to bring Dick a cup of coffee and take over his job.

"Bass, let's go over to a table and talk about your future," Dick commented.

They sat at a nearby table with their coffee and Dick told Bass, "Let me make it very clear to you. There is a good possibility you will wind up in one of two criminal cases. A drug case or a murder case."

"What! What are you talking about? It is the second time you have threatened me."

"We have found the man in the picture I showed you with the Asian woman in Blaine. That woman was possibly involved in killing her husband last night. We can tie you to this man by his activities in this tavern with you," Dick stated strongly.

"I don't have anything to do with those people! I have talked to that man while he was at the bar, that's it," Bass responded.

"The woman sitting by you is an FBI agent, she knows all about your activities. The FBI has been watching you due to you being friends with Bodie and Tweed. Do you want her going into your history with the police? That will send your ass to prison. Now! Where can we find this man you call Tweed, or you can be picked up by the police," Dick demanded.

"Okay, I will tell you all I know. Bodie is a friend from school days. Tweed is my half-brother, and I have very little to do with him. I give him money at times to pay for his moorage fees. If I don't, he will lose his slip and wind up living with me, and I can't have that because he is into drugs," Bass explained.

"Where does Tweed work," Dick asked?

"At times, he gets jobs in the boatyards in town," Bass said.

"Where is this boat Tweed lives on," Susan asked?

"It's on *M* dock, and the name of the sailboat is *Wind-Catcher*," Bass stated.

"Good, thank you, Bass. You've just saved your ass. We will check out what you have told us and get back to you," Dick said as the three left the restaurant.

Back in Dick's car, Dick asked Marty and Susan what they thought about Bass's story.

Marty spoke up, "I think Bass was so scared he wouldn't dare tell a story like that if it wasn't true."

"What do you think, Susan?"

"I think for us to know the truth, we need to check out Tweed and his boat," Susan responded.

"Okay, let's check out the *Wind-Catcher*."

At the Squalicum Marine Office, Dick explained what they were investigating, and that he needed the Harbor Master for help.

The Harbor Master agreed to help, gave Dick the gate combination and said the boat was on the end dock.

The three headed to *M* dock and the *Wind-Catcher*.

They arrived at the end dock slip and found the boat had slipped her lines and sailed away.

"This is a dead-end. Tweed has gone for a sail and maybe to Canada," Dick said.

"Dick, take me back to the Skylark, where my car is. I have to make some phone calls at the hotel," Susan said.

After Susan was dropped off, Dick and Marty headed back to the office to catch up on some paperwork and call Peggy for an update on their investigation.

As Dick and Marty finished working for the day and were closing up the office, Dick's cell phone rang.

"Hello, Officer Steven, you just caught me heading out the door, what's up," Dick asked as he put the phone on speaker?

"I thought you would like to know we found a boat adrift off the northwest side of Battleship Island."

"What's the connection with me," Dick asked?

"The name of the boat is *Wind-Catcher* owned by Tweed, the man in the pictures I showed you," Steven explained.

"Where is the boat now?"

"They are towing it to our station here in Bellingham for the coast guard investigators to search out what happened to the people on board," Steven commented.

"I need to be there when the tow gets to the station, would you give me a call," Dick questioned?

"Sure, and you can give me an update on the Jamie case," Steven responded.

By six o'clock in the evening, the coast guard boat had towed the *Wind-Catcher* back to the station in Bellingham and tied her up.

Officer Steven posted coast guard personnel to stand guard until the investigators arrived the following day.

By ten the next morning, the coast guard investigators had arrived and were boarding the boat to determine what had happened to the captain.

"Dick, Marty and Susan were also there as guests of the warrant officer in charge, and they were allowed to ask questions as the investigation proceeded."

As the investigation did proceed, Officer Steven told Dick he noticed there were signs of a woman on board with the skipper. There were two glasses used with a smudge of lipstick on one glass. There was an aroma of a lady's perfume in the head.

The helm was tied off in a way to send the boat to Canada across the straights and to run aground.

If grounded it would have taken time to get information back to the coast guard, giving the skipper and others time to leave the area.

"Was there anything else on board," Susan asked?

"Yes, a suicide note was left, but the note was written in such a way the investigator believed the writer didn't commit suicide. One other item indicated that they left on another boat; line hung over the side of the *Wind-Catcher* that indicated they had left in a small boat. Lastly, there were no wallets or purses left, and in most suicides, the person leaves ID," Officer Steven stated.

"How do you proceed with this boat," Dick asked?

"For now, this boat is part of the Jamie and Bodie case due to the owner being Tweed. We know Tweed and the Chinese woman are involved in drugs and maybe the killings. This case will stay with the coast guard for now," Steven said.

"Tell us when the boat is turned over to the sheriff's department," Susan directed.

"Sure, as soon as the coast guard investigator is finished," Steven responded.

Dick thanked Officer Steven, and they headed to the office.

While driving toward the office, Susan said she was starting to see that the case may not be a drug case.

"What do you mean, Susan," Dick asked?

She went on to say that she checked with the DEA and found the Asian woman had been in contact with a Mexican person, not the drug cartel. DEA said Chung and Tweed are moving very few drugs, too small for killings. The drug lords in China would not go for killing to put the spotlight on them. They are like bats hiding from the lights.

At the office, Dick asked Susan if she would check with the DEA on the relationship between Bodie, Tweed, and Bass, about moving drugs. He then asked Marty to check with the marina on who insured the *Wind-Catcher* and who was paying the moorage. This information could give them a lead.

"I will stay in the office to make some phone calls, catch up on files and some of our other contracts," Dick affirmed.

CHAPTER 10

DEATH AND DRUGS

There had been a lull for a week in the investigation with no new leads; then Detective Meeks called Dick at home.

Meeks informed Dick that Chung Me Li was arrested on his warrant in a restaurant in San Diego, along with a Mexican individual.

"She will be back in San Juan County Sheriff's Office within a week."

Dick was excited to hear Chung would be back in Bellingham. He was hoping to get answers on Jamie's killer.

"I'll call as soon as Chung arrives here in town," Meeks assured Dick.

Dick acknowledged Meeks and said, "In the meantime, I will continue searching for Tweed, he's in Bellingham hiding. If we get Tweed and Chung in jail at the same time, we will be able to play the two off against each other, and hopefully, the truth will come out."

Dick finished his phone call and was having his dinner when the doorbell rang. *Who in the hell could that be this time of the night?* Dick thought.

At the door Dick could see Susan staring at the peephole. He opened the door, "What's up, Susan, come in?"

"I thought I would come by and tell you what I found out from DEA on the three men, if it's not too late."

"No, come in. Care for a beer, that's all I have besides water," Dick said.

"Yes! It's been a hard day running down those guys' backgrounds," Susan explained.

While Dick went into the kitchen for the beer, Susan sat down on the small couch and looked around Dick's living abode to get a feeling about him. *Depressing*, she thought.

Dick returned with a couple of beers and sat down on an overstuffed chair across from her. "Give me a short version of the boys. I'll read your report later," Dick said.

"Sure, I found Bass was a half-brother of Tweed, which you knew, and Bass has tried to help Tweed get away from drugs. Bass has worked hard trying to get ahead, and he wanted to get away from Tweed's drug use and selling drugs. Bass has no police record.

Bass has been a lifelong friend of Bodie from grade school. They worked hard to have a food truck business but failed due to Tweed getting involved in drug use and disrupting from the food truck. This is where DEA got involved with Tweed.

Bodie is the one who informed DEA about Tweed's selling drugs. One night, Tweed, along with others, was arrested for selling drugs around the truck. Later, Tweed was let out of jail without charge.

Lastly, is Tweed, who has never had a steady job, but the interesting item about Tweed is he always had money. Drugs are all I have found about Tweed," Susan explained.

"What about Bodie and Jamie?"

"Bodie got involved with the NSA through Jamie. Jamie and Bodie worked a lot of times together on their computers. That is where the two of them hacked into the Red Army.

It seems Bodie shared this Red Army information with someone, probably Tweed, and that is where the killing started," Susan explained.

"You've had a great day, Susan. Can I reward you with another beer?"

"Sure, if you will have one," Susan responded.

"Okay, let's," Dick said as he headed for the kitchen.

Susan followed Dick and said, "You don't have to serve me. I can get the beer with you," as she leaned up against the short kitchen counter.

Dick popped open a beer for Susan and one for himself.

"Can I ask you a personal question, Dick?"

"Sure, if it's not too personal," Dick responded inquisitively.

"Have you ever been married?"

"Yes, are you married, Susan?"

"No, I've not had time to get involved."

"Don't you have urges to be with a man to enjoy his type of company," Dick questioned?

"Yes, but in my type of work, I'm on the road most of the time. Sometimes agents will cross paths and have an evening with a drink and dinner," Susan said.

"How about you, Dick, don't you have urges for the company of a woman?"

"I'm the same as you, I do have urges to enjoy a woman's company," Dick responded.

"You said you were married. Where is your wife? Did she leave for another man," Susan asked?

"No, why do you ask?"

"I was just wondering if you knew the wonders of marriage. I noticed your abode is mainly of a man's making," Susan said.

"I was married for ten years to a beautiful and magnificent woman. I lost her a year ago when she passed away from cancer," Dick stated sadly.

Susan could feel the night suddenly get heavy with sadness and discomfort, "I'm so sorry for your loss of your loving partner. Please forgive me for being an ass," Susan said.

"It's been a long day, tomorrow is a big day," Dick responded.

Susan headed for the guest room, and Dick headed for his. The two had a hot, sweaty night from humidity and the subject of Dick's wife.

At daybreak, Dick and Susan were sitting at the kitchen counter having coffee when he said, "Marty will be here soon, and we can plan on finding Tweed."

You said you didn't believe Tweed jumped overboard with the Chinese woman, Chung. You're right, we found Chung. I believe Tweed and Chung left on a small boat to San Juan Island while the sailboat sailed to Canada. We'll find Tweed," Susan said.

"Tweed was starting to earn big bucks with the Mexican drug cartel selling their drugs. Tweed will not go away from that money.

We think Chung Me Li is moving drugs with Tweed. This supports the case of a drug operation," Dick said.

"Did this drug operation grow big enough to cause a killing? I think Tweed isn't the killer. If he is involved, he is working for someone else," Susan stated.

At that moment, Marty came into the kitchen through the back door. "Good morning, you two. How is the day starting out?"

"We were just talking about where we stand in looking for Tweed," Dick replied.

"I thought Tweed was dead," Marty said sarcastically.

"You know better than that. Tweed is in the area, and I believe Bass can tell us where he is," Dick commented.

"I think you're right, Dick, because Bass talked to me last night when I stopped by Skylark for a drink. He said he was between a rock and a hard place and didn't know which way to turn. I asked him what he was talking about. He said I should know due to me working on the case," Marty responded.

"What's his hang-up," Dick asked?

"He wouldn't say any more, but I could tell he needed to talk to somebody," Marty explained.

"Marty, go back to the restaurant as soon as it opens and talk to Bass again. He may be ready to talk after thinking about his troubles and a good night's sleep, and when you're finished talking to Bass, go to the office and take care of the office operations. You will be our control center. As for me, I'm going back to search for Tweed starting with the harbormaster," Dick stated.

"I'll be going to the coast guard station where I can use their computers to search our subjects through the NCIC, immigration, DEA, CIA, and NSA without someone looking over my shoulder," Susan explained.

With their plans in place, the three investigators left Dick's and started to work.

Marty was at the office when Detective Meeks called to inform her that Mrs. Chung Me Li was now in jail in Bellingham.

"She will be in the Whatcom County Jail, not the San Juan County Jail."

Marty thanked Meeks and immediately called Dick to let him know about Mrs. Chung.

Dick said he would talk to her later; he was going to continue talking to the harbormaster about Tweed's boat.

The harbormaster said different people had paid for Tweed's slip for the last six months; they paid in cash. He also said Tweed's boat never left the slip for that sixth month.

"Why do you think that is?"

"I knew Tweed was a master sailor, and he used to go out all the time by himself," the harbormaster explained.

"If Tweed is a master sailor, then he would know how to tie nautical knots?"

"Oh, yes, Tweed could tie most knots, why do you ask that," the harbormaster questioned?

"No reason," Dick said as he stood up and said goodbye.

Dick drove to the sheriff's office to see if he could interview Mrs. Chung.

As he pulled into the sheriff's parking lot, he saw Susan standing by her car.

"What are you doing here, Susan? I thought you were at the coast guard station," Dick said as he stepped out of his car.

"Marty called me about Chung being in jail here. I wanted to be here to also interview Chung," Susan explained.

"Sure, come on in with me, we'll see if Meeks is here to let us talk to Mrs. Chung," Dick suggested.

In the sheriff's office, Meeks greeted Dick and Susan and asked if they were ready to find out what Mrs. Chung had to say.

"Yes," the two responded.

As they walked toward the interview room, Susan suddenly stopped Meeks and Dick and said, "Wait, I need to tell the two of you something about Tweed."

"Sure, what's up," Meeks questioned?

"While I was checking Tweed's background, I found the NSA uncovered that Tweed was making phone calls to the cartel. This information was turned over to the FBI, and the FBI opened up a case to investigate. Tweed is involved in a drug operation, but the phone calls indicate some other illegal activity. The DEA looked into drug involvement while the FBI started looking into the other activities Tweed was into. This is where I come into the case. Tweed is the person I'm interested in," Susan said.

"What is Tweed up to besides drugs, and why didn't you tell me this at the start of this investigation," Dick asked?

"You know as well as I do, I'm not supposed to talk to anyone about the case I'm investigating. I had to be sure who I was working with before I could say anything," Susan explained.

Meeks said with a big smile, "Don't worry about it, Susan, we understand the FBI can be aloof toward other investigators."

CHAPTER 11

ME LI'S STATEMENT

In the interview room, Meeks told Mrs. Chung that Dick and Susan would sit in on the questions about her and Tweed.

"That's fine," Me Li responded.

"Mrs. Chung, I see you have some conditions before we start the interview," Meeks said.

"Yes, my conditions are for the prosecutor," Chung explained.

"What are the conditions," Meeks asked?

"I can give you details if the prosecutor would sign an agreement not to deport me back to China and not charge me," Mrs. Chung Me Li stated.

"Get the San Juan County prosecutor, jailer," Meeks shouted out to the deputy standing outside the room!

Soon the prosecutor entered the hallway.

"I see the prosecutor coming," the deputy responded.

"Tell him we need him now," Meeks stated.

"Okay!"

Within a minute, the county prosecutor was in the room with Meeks asking what was all the rush?

Just then, Susan spoke up, "This may be a federal case. I will listen to Chung's story, inform my boss and he can determine what the FBI can or will do," Susan explained.

"That's fine, but we just need to get Mrs. Chung's statement on paper," Detective Meeks responded.

"Okay, Mrs. Chung Me Li, can I hear what you have to say before the federal prosecutor grants you protection," Susan asked?

"Yes, because I'm innocent of any crime," Chung said.

"Mrs. Chung, let's hear what you have to say,'" San Juan County prosecutor, Mr. Pain, stated.

"Sure, but first, I need one more item, a public defender. I'll need him here to watch out for me so I don't make a mistake," Chung Me Li requested.

By midday, the prosecutor, a public defender for Chung and the federal prosecutor agreed to listen to Chung's statement. If her statement was true, Chung may be able to stay in the States.

"We have lost too much time getting prosecutors and lawyers. Let's take a break for lunch before we start the interview," Meeks explained.

After lunch, all the parties sat down in the interview room and started the interview with Chung Me Li.

Detective Meeks asked Me Li to tell her story about herself, Tweed and the killings of Jamie, Bodie, and her husband, Chung.

Me Li began to tell her side of the story about herself and Tweed.

She explained that she and Tweed did not have a romantic relationship. She worked with him for money through the sale of drugs. About the killings, she never observed anyone being killed while knowing Tweed or anyone else in this area.

As for herself, she was married to Chung Lee Yu for the opportunity to come to the states for the drug lords in China. They wanted her to set up a drug distribution throughout the states.

She stated trouble came when the drug lords wanted to sell the Mexican cartels drugs; in return, they would set up an enforcement unit to influence US politics. The cartel loved the deal and started sending drugs to the northwest.

"Why was that a problem, Me Li," Susan asked?

"The Red Army wanted no part of this drug operation. They felt drugs would jeopardize their operation of information gathering," Me Li said.

"Let's go back to Tweed for just a minute. How were you able to get Tweed into selling drugs," Susan asked?

"I met Tweed through Bodie, a bartender. Tweed came into the bar to push small amounts of drugs and Bodie introduced me. I started talking to Tweed and found out he was selling drugs for the cartel. Later, the cartel gave Tweed more money to work with me," Me Li responded.

"Were the two of you selling a large number of drugs for China and the cartel," Susan questioned?

Me Li had a drink of water, then said, "Once I get an assurance on paper and I am safe, I will give you more details."

The prosecutors agreed and handed the ready to be signed forms to Me Li.

Me Li signed the forms and said, "Okay."

"I'm interested in what you can tell us about the killing of Jamie and Bodie," Meeks said.

"I know nothing about the killing of Jamie or Bodie. I knew Bodie just as a friend through Tweed, and that's it," Me Li stated.

"What else can you tell us about your drug operations, and what did your husband have to do with these drug movements," Susan asked?

"My husband had nothing to do with drugs, and while Tweed and I were building the drug operations, I did overhear some conversation with my husband and his friend. They were talking about building an information network in this area."

"What were the information networks about," Susan asked?

"To be truthful, I don't know," Me Li stated sternly.

"What about the death of your husband? Did this information networks have anything to do with his killing," Susan asked strongly?

"If he was building an informational operation at great cost to the Red Army, why would the army want to kill Chung, the man who was doing the building," Me Li questioned?

"All this killing started when Jamie found out about the Red Army starting something in the States," Susan stated.

"I believe you are right. When Bodie told Tweed that Jamie had found out something, Chung Lee Yu was doing something in

Mexico. The Chinese Army believed Chung Lee Yu was starting to sell drugs from the Cartel and was forced to shut down that operation to protect other operations. Taking no chances, the army had to get rid of Chung Lee Yu," Me Li commented.

"How'd Tweed find out about the conversation," Susan asked?

"I don't know. But, at the same time, the Chinese drug lords believed Chung Lee Yu was building a spy ring. They didn't want to get involved in spying because of me and told me to get rid of Lee Yu," Me Li said.

"You were sent to the States to build drug operations by the drug lords, which had nothing to do with spying, how did the drug lords find out about Chung Lee Yu spying," Susan asked?

Chung Me Li said that Tweed told her about Bodie and Jamie hacking, and she told the drug lords, her boss, and they shut down the drug operations to stay away from the Red Army. Also, Tweed was afraid and told the cartel. They didn't want to get involved in a spy operation and stopped the drug shipments. With the drug shipment stopped by both groups, she thought Tweed felt he had to kill Chung Lee Yu to stop the spying so the cartel would start sending drugs again.

"Okay, then, who killed Jamie and Bodie," Dick asked?

"The army may have had her killed to stop her hacking, or the Mexican Cartel may have killed her thinking she was involved in spying. They both needed to stop her," Me Li responded.

Meeks spoke up, "It's time for a break. Have a female deputy take care of Me Li's needs while we have a time-out. Have the deputy closely protect our witness, the cartel and China knows we have her."

In the break room, the detectives and Agent Tomas sat around and discussed what Me Li had told them.

Susan spoke up and said the FBI would have to take charge of this case because it became a federal threat to the nation, and the DEA would take over the drug operation investigations.

Meeks strongly spoke up, "There has to be some way for the three agencies to work together on this case. I need to close these three killings jurisdictionally.

"I think we can work together. I'll talk to my boss before agreeing on a joint operation," Susan explained.

With the case now at a standstill until Susan obtains the okay, Meeks said, "We can still work the case until a decision is made."

After everybody had left the station, Meeks told Dick and Susan he had something to tell them.

"What's up, Meeks," Dick asked?

"Let's go have coffee, and I'll fill you in on what the coast guard has found," Meeks said as they walked out to his car.

At the Birch Door Restaurant, Meeks told Dick and Susan that the coast guard investigator just found a security tape from an Anacortes Ferry that showed a white Cadillac leaving Anacortes at 1800 hours, heading into the islands the day Jamie was killed.

On another ferry, the next day, the same car was taped leaving Orcus Island for Anacortes. The investigators watched the tape and couldn't tell who was driving the car.

"Could this be our killer," Meeks questioned?

"There is a great possibility. I know who owns that car. It's Clinton Biltmore, who is a friend of Mr. Chung. Clinton and Tweed have both worked on Chung's yacht," Dick said.

Susan spoke up, "Dick, you and Meeks, please hold up on telling anyone about this car until I call my boss to see how we can proceed on this case."

The two men agreed with Susan to wait for one day, and by that time, the coast guard investigator would be finished with the boat.

With the coffee break over and the case discussion completed, the three headed back to the sheriff's parking lot so Dick and Susan could get their cars.

At the parking lot, Dick said to Susan, "We have some free time for the rest of the day. After you make your call, would you like to go for a ride? It's a beautiful day, and we need a break."

Susan looked at Dick with a curious smile and said, "Is this the beginning of a one-night stand?"

"No, this is a much richer experience, this is an old fashioned date where the girl and boy just go for a ride and have a good time," Dick replied with a returning smile.

"Sure, I haven't been on a date like that since high school," Susan replied warmly.

The two settled down in Dick's car.

"Let's go for a ride," Dick responded.

"We need to stop by the coast guard station so I can make the call to my boss."

Soon the two had cleared the station and were on their way to Mount Baker on a sunny day.

Susan found it to be a beautiful ride through the countryside, dotted with small farms and ranches and small farmland. Within an hour, they had driven out of the farmland and started up the winding road into the foothills covered with evergreen and sparkling cold streams. Soon the foothills turned to rocky, rugged mountains covered with tall trees and light snow. Susan felt exhilarated at the energy used to push the car up the winding road.

At the end of their trip, they pulled into a snow-covered parking lot to find the lodge was closed for the evening. Dick was able to find the owner still there, and he gave them coffee and sandwiches for their trip.

The two were much appreciative of the hot coffee and the owner's consideration for letting them have a little picnic on an open deck.

Bundled in heavy blankets loaned to them by the owner, they enjoyed looking out over the valley and hills below, sipping their coffee. They said little and just enjoyed the scene.

Finished with their picnic, they headed down the mountain and through the farmland and on to town.

By ten p.m., the two were back in town and pulled into Dick's driveway.

Dick said, "This was a great drive. Let's top it off with a drink of port."

"No, Dick, take me to the hotel. I can't stay with you tonight, and please don't ask me why," Susan requested.

"Okay, Susan," Dick responded as he backed out of the drive and headed to Bellwether Hotel.

Within a short trip, Dick pulled up in front of the hotel and said, "I hope you are okay, and I hope I didn't do something wrong on our ride."

"No, Dick, you were great, it's me. I need to be by myself," Susan explained.

Dick helped Susan out of the car and walked her to her room. "Good night, I will meet you in the morning at the sheriff's office," Dick explained.

"Sure, thanks for the date, I had a wonderful time," Susan said.

Dick opened her room door and said goodnight.

"Good night, Dick," she replied as she closed the door.

Inside her room, she dropped her purse and jacket on a chair and sat down by a huge window overlooking the bay. Her life had always been just work and fun with men, but with Dick, she found herself relaxed and comfortable while wanting to be with him.

CHAPTER 12

WHERE IS TWEED?

Back home after a great trip with Susan, Dick entered the front door and noticed the red light flashing on his phone. After hanging up his shoulder holster, he pushed the red answer button.

"Dick, this is Marty, call me anytime. Tweed came into the office today and needed to talk."

Dick quickly dialed Marty's phone; there was no answer.

Dick grabbed his revolver and jacket as he ran out the door.

He sped over to Marty's house and thought the shooter had come back to kill her.

He pulled onto Marty's driveway, and Marty pulled up beside him.

"Why are you over here," Marty asked?

"I tried to call you, and you didn't answer your phone. After you were shot before, I was afraid you might have been shot again," Dick explained.

"Come in the house and I will tell you what Tweed said," Marty said.

Inside, the two had a beer, and Marty said, "Tweed came in the office and wanted to get some information off his chest without the police. I told him he could talk to us without the police. Tweed then said that he was talking with Bass at the tavern about what had happened to Jamie and Bodie. Tweed told me, 'Chung Me Li believed her husband, Chung Lee Yu, did the killing. He is the only person who had direct contact with the Red Army, and they would give the order to kill Jamie and Bodie."

"I asked Tweed how he knew this," Marty said. "Tweed told me he was with Chung Lee getting his boat ready for some kind of a trip when he got a phone call. The caller was speaking in Chinese, and when Chung was finished talking, he asked him what was wrong. Chung told him Bodie had done something very bad and he would have to pay for it. He believed the caller wanted him to take care of Bodie."

"That's good information, Marty, but not hard evidence. What else did you find out from Tweed," Dick questioned?

"Tweed told me when Mr. Chung was killed, all money stopped coming in to support him."

"Did Tweed know Chung Lee Yu stopped his operation," Dick asked?

"Tweed told me Mr. Chung was angry when he was told no more money was coming from China because of him calling a Mexican person. That means the Chinese didn't need Mr. Chung Lee Yu or Chung Me Li. Why would the Chinese kill Chung Lee Yu and not Me Li unless she had another job," Marty stated.

"We have to find out if she had another job. Maybe Me Li and her husband were in a spy operation together? Can you find Tweed and see if he will give a statement, and maybe he can tell us about others involved in Chung's operations?"

"I think so," Marty responded.

"I'll see you at the office in the morning, and hopefully, Tweed will come," Dick responded as he left Marty.

The next morning, Dick checked his phone messages and found one from Susan who told him she was headed for the university.

Dick headed for the office, and as he pulled into the parking stall under the office building, an Asian man appeared at his driver's window and, with his revolver barrel, tapped on the window.

"Step out of the car slowly, and turn around and put your hands on the top of the car," the stranger stated firmly.

Dick did what the man said and stood with his hands on the car, waiting for hot lead to bore into his brain; instead, the man said, "I will say this one time, and if I have to come back, you are a dead man. We are tired of you nosing into something you know nothing about. Do you understand?"

"Yes," Dick said.

"You and your partners are irritating big people who are about to smash you like a roach, stop it or die, shithead!"

Dick said he understood as he stood waiting for another demand. Then he heard a car door slam and a car leave the garage. He turned to see the stranger had gone.

Once Dick was back in his office, he sat at his desk and slammed down a shot of bourbon to steady his nerves while he tried to make some sense of his encounter; *This is three times I have been threatened, the next time, I'll surely die.*

The phone rang and Dick slowly picked it up, "Hello."

"Good morning, Dick, this is Meeks. I just got the word from my prosecutor that the federal prosecutor will let the county prosecutor represent them and work a deal with Mrs. Chung Me Li in order to get her statement on paper."

"That's great, when is the interview?"

"This afternoon, I'll call you when I'm ready," Meeks stated.

Dick hung up feeling that they might soon know the killer or hopefully the driver of the white Cadillac that left Orcas.

At 10:00 a.m., Dick left the office and headed for the sandwich shop next door for an early lunch.

Marty came in and sat down with him saying, "What a hell of a day!"

"What's going on, Marty?"

"I can't get Tweed to turn himself over to the police and give them a statement."

"Why won't he do that, it would clear him," Dick commented?

"I told him that, but he said if he reports to the police, the Chinese will find him and Mrs. Chung and kill them. He's going to stay hidden until he feels safe," Marty reported.

"By the way, did Tweed say why he faked his suicide along with Me Li on his sailboat," Dick asked?

"He said, for some reason, Mrs. Chung felt the Red Army was coming after her, and she needed to disappear. She thought a fake suicide would end the Chinese searching for her.

I think this is a game she is playing to keep control over her situation until she can find a way out," Marty responded.

"We will have to wait and see what Susan finds out from the Chinese studies director," Dick suggested.

Dick and Marty walked back to the office, where Dick called Peggy and informed her that he felt they were closing in on the killer of her daughter.

After the phone call Dick said, "Let's take it easy for the rest of the day and let the secretary lock up."

"Yes, we need to get away from this case, and maybe we will see it in a new light tomorrow," Marty stated.

Later, Dick was busy in the kitchen preparing his dinner when the doorbell rang. He looked at the clock on the wall. It showed it was 8 p.m. *Who in the hell could that be? Susan said she will probably stay in Seattle tonight,* Dick muttered to himself as he reached for his revolver.

He walked over to the door and looked through the peephole to see Susan standing there.

He opened the door and said, "Come in!"

Susan stepped in and continued on to the kitchen to pour herself a glass of wine.

"God, Susan, what the shit happened to you? You look mentally wiped out," Dick asked?

"Well, my friend, you're right, I spent a lot of time today with the director of Chinese studies. After promising him a lot of help, he finally told me that one of his visiting speakers from China may be a spy and used his department as a cover, but he can't prove it."

"That is the reason the director hasn't reported this person to the authorities. If what the director says is true, then Jamie's case is a good possibility of a spy operation, and you have just opened up a big can of trouble, Susan."

"Dick, if the director is right, the Chinese probably killed Jamie and Bodie. This means they will kill anyone to keep it quiet," Susan stated.

"That's right, and there were others the Chinese Army will clean out. Jamie and Bodie were just the first," Dick explained.

"I sure hope you're wrong, this is a major problem for the FBI and the CIA," Susan said as she poured another glass of wine.

For the next three hours, Dick and Susan consumed three bottles of Dick's best ten-dollar wine

Finishing the wine, their inhibitions had dropped, and they had become like close friends bragging about each other and drinking.

Dick opened a bottle of brandy, started drinking and before long, they were congratulating each other with a hug. A couple more brandies, a light kiss of congratulations and then a nightcap with one more light kiss became a hot passionate embrace.

The next morning, Dick was having a shower when Susan stepped into the bathroom dressed in a loosely tied bathrobe. It gave Dick a peek-a-boo glimpse of her breathtaking body.

"We can save water showering together," Susan stated.

This action sent Dick into a state of shock. He believed after the big mistake last night, having sex with Susan jeopardized their relationship and quickly stated, "I'm finished," as he stepped out of the shower.

Susan smiled as she watched Dick grab a towel and wrap it around his bare wet ass and hustle out of the bathroom.

Later, as they were having coffee at the kitchen counter, Dick spoke up, "Susan, we made a mistake last night drinking too much and going to bed together, we can do better than that."

With a big smile, Susan had let Dick ramble along, trying to clear up his conduct and guilt.

"Dick! You thought we slept together and made love? Well, let me ease your mind. After drinking too much last night, you went to sleep on the couch. I helped you to bed, then I went to the guest room and to bed. There was no sex. I knew when I stepped into the bathroom, I would put you in shock because you thought we had somehow committed to each other. I just wanted to see you squirm a little, and I sure got a kick out of watching you."

"We are still independent of each other, but someday, that may change, who knows?" Dick said with a smile. "Thank you, Susan, you mean woman. I feel better about it all. But someday, if it is the right time, the right reason, and without booze, who knows."

"Yes! Dick, it has to be right," Susan responded.

"Now, let's get back to work finding a killer," Dick recommended.

Dick and Susan left the house and headed for the office. As they drove along, Dick told Susan about the man who threatened him with a gun in his parking garage yesterday, and that the man was Chinese.

"Chinese, he fits the description that the director gave me as the visiting Professor Ping. Ping may be our killer. Maybe we are getting too close to the spy operation. I think he is trying to run you off instead of killing you. You are working too close to the police. What did he want from you," Susan asked?

"He wanted to scare me away from the case," Dick explained, "but the way he talked to me, I knew he could kill me with a blink of an eye."

As Dick pulled into his parking stall under the building, Susan started looking for any strangers standing around or sitting in a car. With the area clear, Susan relaxed.

The two left the car and took the elevator up to the first floor and to Dick's office.

In his office, Marty was sitting at her desk working. "Good morning, you two," Marty acknowledged them.

"Good morning, Marty, how is your morning starting out," Dick asked as he headed toward the coffee pot.

"Just another day in the neighborhood," Marty responded.

"Well, don't plan on going anyplace. The three of us are going to the sheriff's office to interview Mrs. Chung," Dick stated.

At 9:00 a.m., Meeks called and told Dick the interview would start at ten.

"We will be there."

At ten, Dick and Marty stood by the viewing window next to the interview room. They watched Susan and Meeks as they sat across from Mrs. Chung with their files, questioning her.

"Good morning, Mrs. Chung, are you ready for an interview with us," Meeks asked?

"Yes, but are you sure about my protection?"

"Yes, I'm sure, here is the contract. Now let's start Me Li," Meeks instructed.

"Where do you want me to start, Detective Meeks?"

"Start with when you started the drug operations," Meeks suggested.

"I started in China as a lone fourteen-year-old girl living on the streets of Hong Kong. It was an easy city for a young girl to live in due to so many rich men living there. I took a lot of money from those men by doing them favors."

"How did the drugs come into your life," Susan asked?

"I started using drugs with these rich men while taking their money," Me Li said.

"How did the drug lords get involved with you," Susan asked?

Me Li stopped and had a drink of water, then continued, "I started selling drugs for the drug lords because they were watching these rich men and me."

"Did you ever try to get out of that way of life," Meeks asked?

"No, I was young and having fun living the high life, and when these drug lords offered me to go to the US to start up moving drugs there, I was excited about going to the States. The drug lords didn't wait for my passport, it took too long, so they set me up with a man in the states to marry. I could move to the States quicker."

"Was that man Mr. Chung Lee Yu," Meeks asked?

"Yes, Chung came to Hong Kong knowing he was going to marry me, and as soon as he arrived, we were married," Me Li responded.

"Did you come to Bellingham right after marriage," Meeks asked?

"Yes, as soon as Chung and I arrived in the US, Chung was ordered by the lords to find help in moving drugs. I found Tweed through my husband, who knew Tweed was already pushing drugs. Tweed and I started moving drugs coming from China, and we did well," Me Li explained.

"Did you know Mr. Chung was setting up a spy operation in Seattle at that time," Susan asked?

"I didn't know that. But when Chung Lee started meeting others on a daily basis, I started nosing around. Then Chung found out I was snooping on him. He told me he was helping China, but he would not tell me how," Me Li said.

CHAPTER 13

———

THE FOG IS STARTING TO CLEAR

"What happened to start this killing of Jamie and Bodie," Meeks questioned?

"I'm not sure, I think when Jamie told Bodie she found out about Mr. Chung talking to some unknown in Mexico, the Red Army believed Chung was getting involved with drugs and wanted no part of any drug group," Me Li explained to Susan.

"How did the Chinese find out about Chung talking to someone in Mexico," Susan asked?

"I told the Chinese drug lords what Bodie told Tweed about Jamie's find. I thought the calls were about drugs, but later I found out it was something else. I had to tell the lords about the call, if I didn't, they would have killed me," Me Li said.

"How did this information get to you?" Susan asked.

"This is a very important question, Me Li, go slow," Meeks said.

"Jamie was loading information into the computers for the NSA. She accidentally found Chung contacting someone in Mexico and China. She told Bodie what she found. She then told Tweed, and Tweed told me. I knew if I didn't tell the drug lords, they would kill me for keeping something from them," Me Li stated.

"Why didn't that information stop with the drug lords," Meeks asked?

"The drug lords told the army to save their drug operations," Me Li explained.

"What happened after you told the drug lords," Susan asked?

"That's when the killing started," Me Li stated, confidently.

"Now the most important question, who is doing the killing Me Li," Meeks asked?

"That I can't tell you. Chung Lee would not talk to me about his operations. As for the drug lords, they shut down the drug operation when they found out the Red Army was involved with me through my husband," Me Li explained.

"It sounds like we have come to the end of your part in the killing and drugs. Is there anything you want to add to your statement?"

"You may want to talk to the director of Chinese studies in Seattle, who may know something about Chung," Me Li said.

"What about the director of Chinese studies," Susan asked?

"Chung was always calling the UW. I don't know who he was calling, but the director may know," Me Li responded.

"Thanks for that bit of info, Me Li," Susan commented as she and Meeks stood up and left the interview room.

Back in Meeks's office, Dick said, "It seems to me the drug operation is gone for now, and somebody is killing people off to protect a possible spy operation."

"You're right, Dick, we have got to get with Tweed to find out his side of the story. He may not know anything about spying, he may be just in the drug business," Meeks suggested.

Susan spoke up, "I have to call my boss. I have to make sure about this spy operation so our investigation is going in the right direction. I now believe the drug sales had no part in the killing."

Dick spoke up, "Marty can continue canvassing the areas for any information on Tweed while you and I go back to Skylark for information on Tweed from Bass."

Meeks thanked Dick and Marty for continuing to help him in finding Jamie's killer. Then told Susan he would help her clear up her spy operations. "That kind of Chinese operation could destroy the country," he said.

Outside the station, Dick and Susan told Marty goodbye and be very careful.

After Marty drove off, Susan asked Dick if he would like to go for lunch while she called her boss.

Dick seemed to be excited about spending time with Susan and responded quickly, "I'd like that."

While Dick and Susan were having lunch, Susan called her Boss. When she finished updating him, she explained to her boss that she wanted to stay in Puget Sound to make sure that if there was a spy operation, she'd clean it out and arrest all the people involved.

At the end of their lunch, neither Tweed nor Bass had appeared, so Susan was ready to leave for Seattle. Dick found himself feeling a little lonely about not working with Susan and told her so.

Susan was surprised; *This is all I need now, having feelings for some man I'm working with,* Susan thought to herself as she got into her car for Seattle.

After Susan left, Dick headed for the coast guard station to get updates from Officer Steven.

Officer Steven told Dick that he did have one big item of interest. "Remember, the Cadillac filmed by the ferry security tapes. I found a report filed at the main ferry terminal explaining that a boat deck worker remembered the driver of the Cadillac because it hit a standpipe on the ferry's car deck, causing a slowdown of cars loading. The worker said the Asian man driving was very nervous when asked if he was okay."

"I have another lead to check out, thanks, Steven," Dick said as he stood up to leave. "I'm going to talk to the owner of that Cadillac," he shook Steven's hand and departed.

In Fairhaven, Dick drove into the boatyard and searched for the white Cadillac and Clinton Biltmore. Without luck in finding the Cadillac or Clinton, Dick left the yard and spent the rest of the afternoon searching Bellingham; he didn't find the car.

Dick headed for the office to check on their other contracts.

"Hi, boss lady of the office, how are things going in the office while Marty and I have been out working," Dick asked?

"I'm glad you are here, it's been a busy day with other cases we have contracts with," Linda Lane stated.

"I think you will have to carry the load on these cases because I have to keep working on Peggy's case along with Marty," Dick clarified.

"I can do that, but I want you to keep me updated on Jamie's case, so if I have to help, I'll know where we are in the investigation," Linda responded.

"Don't worry, I'll keep you in the loop," Dick said as he hung up his jacket and shoulder holster.

At 8 p.m., Dick was closing down the office for the day when Tweed walked in.

"I'm here to turn myself in to the sheriff if the sheriff will protect me," Tweed exclaimed.

"That's what we have been waiting on, Tweed, I'll call Meeks," Dick responded.

"Tell the detective the Chinese are looking for me. They want to kill me because I know about the drug movement in the States," Tweed explained.

Dick found Tweed's comment about drugs a little short and questioned him about the spy operation.

Tweed said he knew nothing about spying and asked, "What spying?"

"Okay, Tweed, come in and have a seat, I'll call Detective Meeks, he is heading up the investigation. He will be the one that can put you into protective custody," Dick suggested.

At 8:30 p.m., Meeks arrived and explained to Tweed what he could do for him if he could help put Jamie and Bodie's killers in jail.

Tweed agreed because Bodie was his friend.

At 10:00 p.m., Meeks had listened to Tweed and said, "I need to stop this interview and start an official interview tomorrow at the station. Tweed, I'll put you in lockup for your safety tonight," Meeks advised.

Dick closed the office, and Meeks took Tweed to jail.

In the parking lot, Dick said, "Good night, Meeks. I'll see you tomorrow."

At home, Dick found his front door unlocked. He pulled his .38 from his shoulder holster, slowly walked into the front room, and his eyes quickly focused on Clinton sitting on the fireplace hearth.

"How did you get into my home," Dick commanded as he holstered his .38?

"Your door was unlocked, I just came in to see if you were injured," Clinton stated.

"No, you can't shit me, Clinton, the door was locked. You jimmied the door lock. What do you want," Dick questioned?

"Yes, I did jimmy the door lock. I couldn't stand on your doorstep and wait on you. The word on the street is that you wanted to talk to me about my car," Clinton stated.

"That's right, Clinton."

"I came here to work out a deal with you," Clinton stated.

"Sure, we can work out a deal, if you have information to clear up the killing of Jamie and Bodie," Dick advised.

"What I have will be beneficial," Clinton stated.

"This is going to be a long story, let's wait until tomorrow. I'll see you in my office," Dick said.

"Okay, don't call the cops until after we talk," Clinton suggested.

"That's a deal, see you tomorrow," Dick said as he opened the front door for Clinton.

CHAPTER 14

CHANGE OF COURSE

At 8:00 a.m. the next morning, Dick walked into his office and acknowledged Linda and Marty saying, "Good morning."

Marty responded, "I just made coffee."

"It's strong coffee," Linda exclaimed!

"Good, strong coffee I need. By the way, we are going to have a man come in and give us a statement related to the killing of Jamie, I hope," Dick stated.

"Who is it, and what can he tell us," Marty asked?

"I'm not sure, Marty, what he can tell us, his name is Clinton Biltmore, and he is the owner of that white Cadillac we've been looking for. It's the car that was seen on the day before the killing. It was going to Orcas Island, and it was seen the morning after, driven by an Asian man," Dick said.

"This may be our big break," Marty commented.

"I hope so, we have to find the killer of Jamie and Bodie and get to the bottom of the spy operation for Susan," Dick said.

With his coffee poured, he sat behind his desk and watched Clinton walk in.

"Good morning, Dick," Clinton said.

"Good morning, Clinton, come in and have a seat. This is my partner, Marty, and our secretary, Linda."

"Good morning, Mr. Biltmore, would you like to have coffee," Linda asked?

After being seated and having a cup of coffee, Clinton stated, "Where would you like for me to start in helping you?"

Dick said, "Start with the relationship with you and Chung."

"Our relationship started about two or maybe three years ago. I was working on a boat in the Fairhaven boatyard when Chung came up to me and asked if I would work on his boat. He needed help. He had a forty-two-foot Grand Banks boat. That was the start of our relationship."

Dick responded with, "How did you start using his boat for your trips?"

"For a time, I worked on Chung's boat, and he started asking me to take the boat out on the Bay to keep the drivetrain working in top-notch shape. Next, he wanted to know if I would like to use the boat on short trips."

Then Dick asked, "Why would a person want to let another person use his boat for free that is something boaters don't do?"

"We made a deal. I could use the boat if I kept it up. Chung would buy the parts, and I would do the work."

"That makes sense, but what's with the car arrangement," Dick asked?

"I felt uneasy about him wanting to use my classic car when he had two cars himself. I asked him why he wanted to use my car instead of his own, plus he kept it full of gas. He told me he loved driving my classic car. It made him feel good."

Dick queried, "Where does Chung's wife come into play, Clinton?"

"She came from China as Chung's wife, and I was introduced to her as soon as she settled into Chung's home on Chuckanut Drive. I never had much to do with her, and she wasn't interested in knowing me."

"What's with Chung's wife driving your car," Dick asked?

"Chung did ask me to let her drive my car because she loves driving that big convertible. I didn't want her to drive it, but Chung had done so much for me, and as a friend, I agreed. Now that's all I can tell you about her," Clinton explained.

"Now, the important part, the killing of Jamie," Dick stated.

"I don't know who killed Jamie and Bodie. I know neither Tweed, nor I killed them. I was with Tweed on Chung's boat, and I can prove it. The coast guard boarded the boat in Friday harbor at four in the morning looking for drugs," Clinton explained. "I pointed to my picture on the boat that night with Tweed."

"When I first showed you the picture, you said you didn't know who the one person was, that one person was you, and the other one is Tweed. Why did you lie to me before?" Dick asked.

"At the time you showed me the picture, I could see you didn't recognize me in the picture. I didn't know why you were looking for me. I just wanted to get away from you and your investigation," Clinton explained.

"Did Mr. Chung ever ask you to help move drugs?" Dick asked.

"No, but he did ask me interesting questions. He asked me how I felt about all the military in the area, and later, he asked if I understood the Chinese government. I told him I didn't care about the Chinese government."

"Did this feeling ever change with you?" Dick asked.

"Yes. On the day Chung was killed, I was at Chung's house discussing a job on the boat when a man came to the house. Chung asked me to wait in the study. I overheard a man arguing with Chung about Chung not working hard enough in setting up his operations. I didn't hear what the operation was. This man told Chung the Chinese government wanted an update on a new item the company was working on. At this time, I knew Chung was involved in something bad," Clinton commented. "Chung responded angrily in Chinese. The unknown man shouted something at Chung. Next, I heard a gunshot ring out, and the front door slammed shut. I ran out of the study and found Chung staggering toward the stairs. I told him I would call an aid unit. He said no, he didn't want the police involved. I followed Chung upstairs to the bathroom, where he died. I left before Me Li, his wife, came home," Clinton stated.

"Now we know Chung was killed by some unknown Chinese man. We know you had an alibi with Tweed when Jamie and Bodie were killed, and the testimony of Me Li cleared her, or so she wants us to believe. Who does this leave," Dick asked?

"One more question, Clinton, who had your car on the night Jamie was killed?"

"It was Mr. Chung, he needed the car to take Me Li to dinner. It was a special night," Clinton explained.

"So Chung killed Jamie, if that's true, why?"

"Maybe Chung found out they had done something bad to him, and he needed to kill them," Clinton commented.

"That's what we are trying to find out. It's time to call Detective Meeks, and for you to give him a statement," Dick explained.

"Wait a minute, there is an unknown killer still out there to kill anyone he feels is a threat to him," Clinton stated.

"I know, Clinton, we have to see what Meeks can do. After he hears your statement he may protect you.

Have another cup of coffee while I call Meeks. I think he can help you," Dick responded.

By noon, Meeks and a court stenographer had arrived at Dick's office and were introduced to Clinton Biltmore.

Meeks informed Clinton he was interviewing him in Dick's office because he didn't want the killer seeing Clinton at the police station. That would look bad for Clinton.

Clinton agreed.

The five sat down, and the stenographer set up her equipment and they started recording Clinton's statement.

For two hours, they questioned Clinton about his work with Chung and any other information he had pertaining to Mrs. Chung's operations.

At the end of Clinton's statement, Meeks took him into custody for his protection.

Later, Dick and Marty left their office for late lunch at a restaurant across the street and discussed Clinton's statement.

In their discussion, Marty questioned where they were going to go now that Clinton had made a useless statement pertaining to

Jamie's death. Tweed and Me Li were in jail, and their last suspect, Mr. Chung, was dead.

Dick responded, "We will have to depend on Susan's information, and we should think about reinterviewing Mrs. Chung. If you remember, Chung Me Li was the name of a guest speaker at the UW some time ago. We haven't questioned her about that time."

"I'm starting to believe Mrs. Chung Me Li could have been at the UW as a guest speaker to recon the Puget Sound area to set up a spying operation," Marty commented.

"That's a great point, and if true, she may be the main player of this spy operation," Dick said.

After eating, Dick and Marty spent their time in the office handling paperwork and phone calls until six.

They closed the office and headed to their respective homes.

At eight, Susan came to Dick's home and interrupted his usual TV dinner and his five-dollar bottle of wine.

"Where is the wine? I need a drink," Susan said as she walked into the kitchen.

"In the fridge. It seems like you had a hard day," Dick commented.

"You're right, I've collected too much information. I don't know where to start with it," Susan explained.

"Well, Susan, start with a glass of wine. Once settled down, take the first item of information you found and determine if it is a piece of the puzzle or something to use later," Dick said.

"Dick, the problem is I don't know what was true and what was bullshit. I'll have to clear each piece," Susan explained.

"Have a drink and wind down while I finish my dinner. Have you eaten," Dick asked?

"Yes, I ate on my way up from Seattle. I knew what you would have to eat, TV dinner," Susan responded with a smile.

Dinner finished, the two sat in the living room with their wine; Susan began to tell Dick what she had found out at the university.

She said the director believed the Chinese guest lector, Dr. Ping, was some kind of a Chinese government agent.

I talked to others in the department who think the guest lector, Dr. Ping, was just fine, and they said he loved America.

Throughout the day, other Chinese names had come up to be suspicious people. But no one knew anything for sure.

"You are in a snake pit at the UW, Susan. Now that we have no suspects here in Bellingham, I should go with you to Seattle and see if I can help you," Dick said.

"No, Dick, you have to stay here and keep searching for some leads on our guest lector, Dr. Ping, who may try to get to Canada or try to kill one of the subjects Meeks has in jail. You also have to give Peggy updates. That is what she's paying you for. I will ask my boss for help," Susan explained.

"I guess you're right, we have to be sure the killer doesn't go free to Canada," Dick stated.

"Now that we've cleared up that problem, can I stay with you tonight? I don't want to drive back to Seattle," Susan asked with a slight smile, knowing Dick wanted to sleep with her.

"Sure, as long as you sleep in the guest room," Dick responded with the same little smile.

As the two finished their wine and headed for bed, it was easy to see a strong feeling building between them, and that a time of reckoning may come someday.

CHAPTER 15

FOCUSING ON PING

After a restless night, Dick and Susan sat in the kitchen and had coffee when Susan said that she believed the man she was looking for was the man that killed Jamie and he was an assassin assigned to protect a spy operation. The killing started with Jamie after she fractured the protection of the operation.

Dick agreed and said he would contact border patrol and the local law enforcement to watch for Dr. Ping, who may be heading for Canada.

By eight, the two were out the door, Susan to Seattle and Dick to his office.

Later, in the office, Marty asked, "What do we do now?"

"I'll ask Meeks if I can go to Chung's home and recheck the place for a missed clue about Chung's killing. I also want to advise Meeks on Susan's thoughts about Dr. Ping."

Marty agreed, and said she would stay in the office to work.

At Meeks's office, Meeks listened to Dick's plans and agreed to let him go back to Chung's house.

Dick thanked Meeks and left for Chung's place, but before he left the parking lot, he called Marty and asked her if she had time to canvas areas around the Skylark restaurant and tavern for Ping; a location Ping knew Tweed visited at times and where Bass worked. Dick told Marty that Ping may try to kill Bass to get to Tweed.

"Sure, and if I see Ping, I'll call the police and you," Marty responded.

At Chung's place, Dick broke the police's blue line tape and entered the front door. Inside, he found the house eerie, quiet, and cold with a copper musky smell of death. He looked for someplace to start searching for that one clue to lead him to Chung's killer and help Susan's case.

Dick spent an hour on the second floor and he found nothing to help. He started down the stairs and made sure he didn't hold on to the fingerprint powdered handrail.

On the first floor, he walked into the study and started his search, and again, he found nothing. Tired of finding nothing, he leaned against a cold fireplace mantel to think about his next search.

In front of him on the mantel, he noticed a very unusually carved pipe holder. He picked it up to admire its craftsmanship. He turned it over looking for where it was made. A burned-in brand: "Made in China", "Ming Me Li Company."

The name Ming Me Li jumped out at Dick, *What the hell is this?*

He then called Officer Steven at the coast guard station and asked him to check Interpol on the company Ming Me Li. This may not be anything, but he thought it may be something.

Officer Steven agreed, and he contacted Interpol through the coast guard investigators.

Dick placed the pipe holder in a plastic evidence bag and tagged it. He continued searching and noticed two books on an end table titled *The Art of Knot Tying* by Gobi Horsemen and the other book named *England's Horsemen Art of Knots*. Dick bagged and tagged these two books and continued searching until he had checked every inch of the house.

Outside, Dick searched the area around the house and found a .380 AUTO handgun at the end of a downspout rain gutter. He bagged and tagged it.

By now, it was the end of the day, and Dick headed back to the office to see what Marty had found out to compare their notes.

At the office, Dick found Marty talking on the phone with someone. After she hung up, she said, "Steven has information for you, and he will talk to you tomorrow."

Marty and Dick shared information and planned to meet the next morning with Steven.

They locked up the office and departed for the day.

Early the next morning, at the office, Dick called Officer Steven to see what he had found out about the Chinese company Ming Me Li.

Steven informed Dick that Interpol found no company of that name now or in the past. Interpol believed this was a cover name used by the Chinese government to hide information.

Dick thanked Steven for his help and said he had some evidence to show him. He would stop by later.

By 10:00 a.m. Dick and Marty stopped by the CG station. Dick showed Steven the pipe stand with the words Ming Me Li on the bottom. He replied that Interpol believed Me Li was a code to pass along the info to agents in Puget Sound and that China was sending Chung Lee Yu the name of their new boss.

Steven looked over the pipe holder, and the name burned on the bottom and said, "Dick, you may be right."

Dick then showed Steven the two books about Gobi Horsemen and English Horsemen special knots.

Steven stated the knots found on Jamie and Bodie were the same as the knots shown in the Gobi book.

"I believe Chung Lee Yu may be the killer," Steven explained.

Dick said he had one more item to show Steven, and that was a .380 auto handgun found in a house gutter downspout. He believed this was the gun that killed Chung but he would know more when Meeks completed the gun testing.

"I can understand why the detectives didn't find the gun in the downspout. The downspout is made of steel, the same metal as the gun. That's why the magnetometer didn't find it," Dick explained.

"Well, Dick, I think the tobacco pipe stand and the books are good support evidence. If the killing of Chung was done by the .380, then we need to find the owner of the gun," Steven explained.

"As for the .380, I just hope we are lucky enough to find prints," Dick commented.

"We will have to see where this takes us."

Dick and Marty said goodbye and headed to see Meeks.

At Meeks's office, Dick gave Meeks the items found at Chung's house for the possible use of evidence.

Meeks took the items to be processed in the lab for later court use, if they proved to be usable.

"Dick, I think the video found on the Orcas Island Ferry of the Asian man driving a Cadillac the morning after Jamie was killed is about as conclusive evidence as we can get," Meeks stated.

"Yes, and I think that Chung Lee Yu was killed by Dr. Ping. Dr. Ping and Chung were friends, but in the world of spies, friendship is out the window," Dick concluded.

"That's cold. A man to be a friend one minute and kill him the next," Meeks responded.

"Are you going to close the files on the Jamie and Bodie case with the evidence you have?"

"No, I'm going to keep the file open just in case something comes in from Susan's case," Meeks stated.

"That's good, I think Susan may bring something to the table when she comes back from Seattle," Marty indicated.

"Marty and I will head back to the office and clean up some paperwork. I'll see you later," Dick said as he and Marty walked out.

Back in the office, Dick called Peggy to update her about who may have killed her precious daughter.

Peggy listened to the gruesome report and then asked how sure he was about who did the killing. "Was it Ping?"

Dick said, "I am 90 percent sure from the evidence found by CG investigators and the evidence in the sheriff's office, but the sheriff isn't going to close the case yet."

Peggy thought for a short time, then said, "Dick, I have the money to keep you working until Jamie's case is closed by the sheriff's office. Can you stay with the case for me?"

"Yes, I will stay with you, even if we run out of money," Dick assured her.

With his phone calls made and time to close, Dick informed Marty, "Lets' go home."

Marty agreed, and the two locked up and headed out for the basement garage.

Dick sat in his car and watched Marty drive out onto the street. He started to leave when he noticed Susan walking up to him.

"Hi, big boy, how about a date," Susan asked?

"Sure, I think I have two TV dinners at home," Dick commented with a smile.

"Sure, do you have wine to go with those expensive dinners?"

At home, Dick and Susan settled down at the kitchen table with a bottle of red wine and a couple of grilled cheese sandwiches.

Susan started explaining what happened in her investigation in Seattle, and said that her boss assigned one agent to assist her. For now, the new agent had been following Dr. Ping around Seattle to get a handle on his daily activities. The day had been dull for the new agent, except for one interesting phone call made by Ping at the Farmer's market.

Dr. Ping had made the call to Mexico. Susan had the NSA and CIA search the call, and so far, they found the call had gone to an unknown person at a transporting company moving goods to and from China.

"This is a great lead. Is the CIA going to continue to assist the FBI in running down the transport agent in Mexico," Dick asked?

"Yes, the CIA is working with Mexico's agents as we speak, and the FBI is investigating whether or not there is a connection between this transport company and any company in the States," Susan responded.

"By the way, what is the name of this lecturer, Ping," Dick asked?

"His name is Ping Me Fat, and that is a name I've never heard of. It could be a cover name," Susan explained.

"What's next, Susan?"

"It looks like I will be focusing on Ping and his operations," Susan explained as she poured them another glass of wine.

"You're on the right path. Meeks and I went through the files, and the evidence is pointing us to Ping," Dick stated with some confidence.

"It looks like Ping is the killer, but is he the main operator over the spy operation," Susan questioned?

"I think so. You can head for Seattle tomorrow."

Susan agreed, "Yes, I'll be pushing the director about Dr. Ping."

"Now that we had a great dinner with wine, why don't we go to bed and get a good night's sleep," Dick advised.

"Right, tomorrow is going to be a long day, and I may not be able to come back to Bellingham in a while," Susan responded.

Dick was nearly asleep when he heard the water running in the bathroom and went to see if there was some trouble.

As he entered the bathroom, he could see Susan in the shower. She didn't see him standing there. He quickly backed out of the bathroom and went back to bed.

Dick laid on his bed and thought about seeing Susan in the shower. The image of her slim, curvy, body and her wet, long, red, hair laying tight against her back bothered him. He was having trouble getting to sleep. *That image of Susan will kill me,* he thought to himself as he punched up his pillow.

"No use, the pillow was still hard." Dick could not sleep.

The shower stopped running.

Dick could hear Susan's floppies walk slowly over to his bedroom door and stop.

For the first time since his wife passed away, Dick found himself aroused at the thought of Susan coming to him.

Then he heard Susan walk on, toward her room.

After a torturous night of trying to sleep, the two were sitting at the kitchen counter when Dick said, "Last night, I heard you finish your shower, come by my door and stop, then walk on. That was the right thing you did."

"To be honest with you, Dick, I was just about to agree with Mother Nature and come into your room," Susan responded.

"That decision we will always question," Dick said with a smile.

The subject was left hanging for further discussion.

"Dick, when I leave today, I don't know when I will be able to get back to Bellingham, and you can't come to Seattle and blow my cover," Susan said warmly.

"I know, you will have to call me when the time is right."

"It's time for me to go. I will call you," Susan said.

After Susan left, Dick sat for a time feeling a sense of belonging and a strong warm feeling of a need to protect Susan. These feelings he had not felt since his wife died.

Suddenly, fear struck Dick. He had to find the evil man coming, now, after Susan.

CHAPTER 16

WHERE DOES DICK GO FROM HERE?

Later that morning, Dick was at his office trying to find a way to help Susan. His first thought was to go to the jail and talk to Me Li in hopes of finding a lead to Ping.

"Marty, you and Linda can take care of the office. I'm going to the jail to talk to Me Li. Her husband may have told her something about Ping, or she may have overheard something they talked about," Dick explained.

"Okay, I need to make some calls and tie up a couple of loose ends on Clinton," Marty responded.

Dick left the office and headed for the jail. He believed Me Li knew more than she wrote in her statement. She never talked about Ping. There is a possibility she may be part of Chung and Ping's operations.

At the jail, Dick met with Meeks in his office and told him he believed Me Li might be part of the spy operation because she had never been questioned to any depth. He would like to interview her one more time.

Meeks agreed with the interview, believing Dick could be right.

Within half an hour, Me Li sat in an interview room waiting for Dick to discuss something.

Dick walked in and sat down across from her and asked if she needed something to drink: water, coffee, or tea.

"No, I'm fine. Why am I here, I've told you all I know about the killing of Jamie and Bodie?" Me Li questioned.

"Me Li, I'm here to ask you some questions about your husband. I believe he was working with someone setting up an illegal operation and they may have killed him," Dick said.

"I don't know anything about an operation, and I didn't care about Chung. I married him because I needed him," Me Li said.

"I know, Me Li, I just want to ask questions about Chung's life, for example, what did he do for a living? Where did he come from in China? Questions like that."

"Oh, that's no problem. I will tell you what I know," Me Li said.

"Good, Me Li, my first question is when did Chung Lee first come to the States, and where was his port of entry," Dick questioned?

"Sure, Chung Lee Yu came to the States around four years ago to Seattle as an export/import agent for a Chinese company. Shortly after coming to Seattle, he moved to Bellingham to be closer to Vancouver to be an export agent for Vancouver shipping also," Me Li explained.

"That's great, Me Li, now I know a little more about him. Can you tell me what company he was working for?"

"I'm not sure, he never would talk about his work. I think he was working with a company called the Ming Company," Me Li said.

Applying a little pressure and taking a fifty-fifty chance in screwing up, Dick told Me Li a lie. He told her she had a problem.

"What kind of a problem," Me Li questioned?

"I talked to a person at the university who knew you and that person said she saw you talking to a man by the name of Dr. Ping Lee Fat," Dick said.

That name shocked Me Li for a moment and she said nothing. Then said, "Chung had a friend in Seattle, a Dr. Ping.

I wanted to meet this man to find out what he and Chung were working on. I called him for a meeting, and I did go to the university to talk to him."

"What concerned you about the name Ping," Dick asked?

"I overheard Chung talking over the phone to a man. I asked Chung who he was talking to. At first, he wouldn't tell me until I pushed him. Then all he would say is the name Dr. Ping," Me Li explained.

"Was Dr. Ping an import agent too?"

"I don't know what Ping did. Chung Lee Yu would not talk about him. He would only say he was a friend," Me Li said.

At this point, Dick started pressuring her to see if she would make a slip-up that Susan could use.

"No, Me Li, this person witnessed you and Ping together at the student union building having coffee. What were you two talking about? Don't lie," Dick explained clearly and slowly.

Again, Me Li said nothing. She searched Dick's eyes for the truth, then she changed the subject and said, "Susan isn't here, so I didn't lie to her."

"Susan is in the other room. She is watching you through the one-way mirror."

Dick noticed she was very uncomfortable and said he had to go out of the room for a minute.

Me Li said nothing and just continued looking up at Dick with a questioning face.

Dick walked into the interview room where Meeks was watching. "What do you think, Meeks," Dick asked?

"I think you may be onto something, Dick. She looks like she was stressed to the point that she may talk to save her ass. Why don't you tell Me Li that Agent Susan Tomas went to verify what she said? We will clear up this mess tomorrow," Meeks stated.

"Good idea," Dick said and returned to the interview room.

"Me Li, Agent Tomas is now verifying what you said. She will be here tomorrow to clear up this matter," Dick stated.

Me Li said nothing.

"Jailer, take Me Li back to her cell," Dick stated.

Dick thanked Meeks and said he would see him tomorrow, and hopefully, Susan would make it.

Later at the office, Dick called Susan to see if she could come up tomorrow to interview Me Li. Me Li might have something to say about Ping and his job.

Susan answered Dick's call and told him her assistant would watch Ping, and she would leave early and hoped to be at the sheriff's office by nine.

Dick thanked Susan and said, "See you tomorrow."

Later at home, Dick sat down on a kitchen stool and had himself a ham sandwich with a beer, feeling lonely and restless.

He needed to get out of the house to shake his feelings and headed for the Waterfront Tavern in the old town, one of his favorite places. He needed to talk to older friends who had seen the town grow: except for a young man he had a beer with a few times; the DC sniper, a madman who would be arrested later for killing innocent subjects walking by in DC.

At the tavern, Dick sat at the bar and had a drink. Windy, the bartender approached and asked, "Dick, what's wrong with you, you seem sad tonight?"

"I don't know, Windy. I think it's the case I'm working on."

"No, Dick, I've seen many sad faces in this bar, and they all end up being a love situation," Windy said with a smile as she wiped off the bar in front of Dick.

Dick downed his drink and started to leave when he noticed Bass walk in and head toward him. Bass sat down on the stool by Dick. "Can I buy you a beer?"

Somewhat surprised to see Bass in this area, Dick settled back down on his stool and said, "Sure, what are you doing here? Isn't this out of your area, Bass," Dick asked?

"Yes, I was looking for you."

"What for? Did you find some information about the killing of Jamie," Dick asked?

"Yes, I did.

Bartender, two beers, please," Bass shouted!

"Okay, I'll have a beer with you and listen to what you have to say," Dick acknowledged.

Windy slid two frosty mugs in front of the two men.

Bass picked up his beer and said, "Cheers."

"And cheers to you, Bass," Dick responded, kindly.

"I have an item I believe will shed light on Jamie's death," Bass stated.

"What is that light, Bass?"

"It is a comment Tweed made at the bar with me," Bass said.

"Wait a minute, why are you telling me this now and not earlier in these investigations," Dick asked?

"Now that Jamie's case is over for Tweed, and he is going to jail, I want to help him by helping you and Meeks in his sentencing," Bass said.

"Okay, what do you have," Dick asked?

"Tweed told me he was worried about Me Li. She was not giving him any drugs to sell, but she was still receiving a lot of money from somewhere. Tweed asked Me Li where she was getting the money, and she said it was money she had saved. He thought she was working on something else for the Chinese government," Bass related.

"Does Tweed have any proof to back up that statement," Dick asked?

"A week later, Tweed asked Me Li about the incoming money again. She let it slip that she was receiving money from Mexico and didn't need the drug lords anymore. He overheard Me Li talking to a man named Ping many times."

"What's Tweed's conclusion about Me Li and Ping?"

"Tweed said he had seen Me Li with a Chinese man a couple of times in Boulevard Park after the death of her husband. Tweed now thought she was replacing her husband, whatever that meant," Bass replied.

"You may be right, Bass. Will you tell Agent Tomas and Detective Meeks? They are the ones that can help Tweed?"

"Sure, if it will help Tweed. He is only guilty of selling drugs, nothing more. I'm afraid for Tweed," Bass replied.

"I'll get back to you after I talk to Agent Tomas. Thanks for the beer," Dick said as he left the tavern.

Dick looked at his watch, showing that it was nine. He called Susan to tell her about Bass's statement, and that she would need to have the time to interview Bass along with Me Li tomorrow.

She agreed and said good night.

CHAPTER 17

TIGHTENING OF THE NOOSE

Five o'clock the next morning came quickly for Dick, he finished getting ready and found himself excited about Susan's interview with Me Li. He was in hopes of finding Jamie's killer.

At the station, Dick walked into Meeks's office and said he was ready to see if Me Li would tell Susan about the activities with her husband and Ping.

Dick told Meeks he had talked to Bass, Tweed's half-brother, who said that Me Li may have taken over Chung's job as the person building a spy operation, or maybe she was the lead agent from the start.

Her background showed the Red Army had her marry Chung, not the drug lords, just to get her in the States quickly. But before her marriage the Chinese gave the university big money to let her lecture at the school of Chinese studies.

This could have been a chance for her to recon the Puget Sound to set up a spy operation.

"So you think the pipe stand with Me Li engraved on the bottom is a way to let Chung Lee know who was coming to be his boss," Meeks questioned?

"Something like that, it would be easy for Chung, an export or import man, to receive information from China through messages like the pipe stand," Dick explained.

Within minutes, Dick and Meeks sat across from Me Li in an interview room.

Meeks being the official person until Susan arrived, said, "Good morning, Me Li, how are you feeling this morning?"

"I'm doing okay for the situation I'm in."

"Would you like to have some coffee to make you feel better?"

"Yes, coffee would be good."

Once Me Li had her coffee, they exchanged pleasantries.

Dick asked, "Are you ready for a conversation about Chung Lee Yu, to find his killer?"

"Yes, let's start. But where is this FBI Agent? Isn't she supposed to be with you for the interview," Me Li asked?

"She will be here soon. I am just getting the opening statements out of the way until she comes," Meeks responded.

Half an hour had gone by in the interview, and Dick was starting to worry about Susan.

"Excuse me, I'll be back in just a moment," Dick advised.

Both Dick and Meeks left the room.

Meeks asked, "Have you heard from Susan?"

"No!

I've got to get ahold of her," Dick said.

Outside the station, Dick called Susan.

The person who answered her phone wasn't Susan, it was her assistant, David Warren, who told Dick that Susan was in the hospital and that she had been shot last night in the school of Chinese studies. She had gone there to meet a man.

"I need to talk to her," Dick stated.

"Sorry, sir, Susan is in an induced coma to keep the swelling down in her head," the assistant explained.

"Did the police catch the man who shot her?"

"No, the police didn't find out about Susan being shot for half an hour or so. A janitor found her lying on the floor in the director's office and called the police."

"Where is Susan?"

"She's at the UW Hospital," the assistant said.

Dick thanked the assistant and said he would call him tomorrow to see how Susan was doing. He called Marty at the office and told her what had happened to Susan, and that he was heading to Seattle after he talked to Meeks.

He also told Marty she would have to run the office with Linda and work on other cases to keep money coming in to pay the bills. He may be in Seattle for some time.

Marty said she understood and not to worry.

Dick finished his call with Marty, called Meeks to tell him what had happened to Susan, and said he was going to Seattle to see what he could do.

Meeks understood, and he would return Me Li to her cell after he talked to her.

At five o'clock, Dick was in a hotel in the U district where he phoned Susan's assistant to see how Susan was doing.

The assistant said Susan was still in a coma, but in the morning, the doctors may be able to bring her out of the coma due to the brain-swelling reducing quicker than they figured.

Realizing he could not just sit and wait, Dick headed to the university police to see if he could obtain information on Susan's shooting incident.

At the police station, Dick introduced himself as Private Detective Dickson Diamond working on a case with Agent Tomas. He asked the desk sergeant if he could speak to the detectives investigating Susan's shooting.

The sergeant made a call to the detective division to inquire if the detectives working the shooting case were there. The sergeant hung up the phone and said a detective would be out to see him.

Soon, a young, well-dressed detective came out to the front office, introduced himself as Detective Ross Carter and asked Dick what he could do for him.

Dick introduced himself to Detective Carter, said he was working on a case with Agent Tomas and would like to know what the Detective could tell him.

Carter questioned Diamond about the case that Agent Tomas and he were working on as they walked back to Carter's desk. There, the two looked at the file that showed Susan was shot in the head at close range with a .22 caliber handgun. The round went under the scalp and around the right side of her head, not entering the skull.

"The doctors said this shot sent a heavy shock into Susan's head, bruising the brain, and the brain started to swell. Susan should be fine in a short period of time," Carter continued.

"Who did the shooting?"

"At this point, we don't know. There wasn't a witness, and by the time the police were notified, the shooter was gone. We will have to wait until we can interview Susan to see what she can tell us," Detective Carter explained.

"Can I be there when you interview Susan," Dick asked?

"Sure, we'll have to wait until the doctors tell us it's okay."

"Detective Carter, could I have a pass of some kind to allow me into the crime scene to look around?"

Carter made a couple of calls and said, "The crime scene investigators are about to finish, when they are finished, you can go in." Carter handed Dick a pass and said, "Be sure I get this back when you are finished."

"Sure, I'll head up to the Chinese department," Dick stated.

"I'll let you know if things change," Carter responded.

At the Chinese studies department, Dick crossed the police line and started looking around for that one item to give him a lead.

After a long time nosing around, he gave up and noticed the morning sun lighting up the room. He began to leave when a young Asian lady walked in.

Startled at seeing police tape blocking the doorway, she blurted out, "What happened in here?"

"There was a shooting in this office last evening. Are you a student here," Dick asked?

"Yes, I am, I've been a student for two years."

"What are you doing here so early in the morning," Dick asked?

"I'm the person that opens the office in the morning."

Taking a chance on finding out who Ping is, Dick said, "Maybe you can help me. No one seems to have a picture of a guest lector from China. I think his name is Dr. Ping. Would you know where I could find a picture of him," Dick asked?

"I've taken a lot of pictures of Chinese students to show my friends back home. Would you like to see if I have a group picture with Dr. Ping?"

"Yes," Dick said with the anticipation of finding out what Dr. Ping looked like.

The lady scrolled through her phone pics until she found one. "Yes, here is a group picture with him."

Dick took the phone, and the young lady pointed to an Asian man standing in the background of the picture. "This is Dr. Ping," she said.

"Do you know what Dr. Ping's full name is," Dick asked?

"His name is Professor Ping Me Fat.

"Can you send me that pic on my phone? I would like to show it to the woman who was shot last night," Dick said.

"Sure, I hope it will help."

"By the way, my name is Dickson Diamond, I'm a private detective. What is your name?"

"My name is Chung Young Yi."

"Could you be related to a man name Chung Lee Yu who was killed a week ago," Dick asked?

"Yes, but I didn't get along with him. He is my uncle, and he paid for my school," Young Yi explained.

"Thank you, Young Yi, for your help," Dick said as he left her standing in the office.

Back at the university police station, Dick returned the police pass to Carter and went back to the hotel.

At the hotel, Dick called to check on Susan. The nurse said Susan was asleep and that Dick could call tomorrow.

CHAPTER 18

DOWN TO ONE

The following morning, Dick left his hotel and headed to the university police to see if he could work out something with Detective Carter to keep him up to date on Susan's condition.

On his way, he stopped by the university hospital to check on Susan. There he met Susan's assistant, Agent David Warren, who had stayed at the hospital to watch over his boss.

"How is she doing this morning, David," Dick asked?

"The doctors said she is doing fine, and the swelling has gone down. They will bring her out of her coma sometime this morning."

"Good news, we need her back," Dick acknowledged.

"In the meantime, Dick, will you go to the police and see what you can find out about the shooter," David suggested.

Dick agreed and left the hospital to see Detective Carter.

As Dick drove to the station, Marty called him on his cell phone. "What's up, Marty?"

Marty explained that Detective Meeks called and informed her that Me Li and Tweed gave a complete statement about their part in the drug dealing. Me Li opened up a little bit on the spy operations. She said, "It's going to be quite a story if we can get her to talk more."

"That's great news, Marty, I'll tell Susan when she wakes up."

At the station, Dick met with Detective Carter in his office, where he showed a video of Dr. Ping leaving the building at the

Chinese studies location around the time Susan was seen going into the building. Carter explained, "What's interesting, after the crime scene team left the area, the video showed Dr. Ping returning to the office. He later left again, this time, with some lady."

"Where is Dr. Ping now," Dick asked?

"He has dropped out of sight."

"I know where he is going, he's going to Bellingham to kill a couple of people before heading for Canada," Dick explained.

"I'll call the state patrol and the border patrol to pick Dr. Ping up if they see him," Detective Carter responded.

"Good, I'll be on my way back to Bellingham, and I'll also contact Agent David Warren and tell him I'm going to Bellingham to find her shooter. David is to stay with Susan day and night. Dr. Ping may come for her if he finds out she is still alive," Dick advised.

Back on the road to Bellingham, Dick called Marty and advised her what had happened and to pass the information on to Meeks to be on the lookout for Dr. Ping. He may be on his way to the Canadian border.

Within a couple of hours, Dick was back in his office, talking with Marty about the best action to find Dr. Ping.

"I believe Dr. Ping will try to kill Me Li before he runs to Canada, where other spies will help him get back to China," Dick commented.

"Before we go too far, would you like to know what happened at Detective Meeks's interview with Me Li?"

"I'm sorry, Marty, I was carried away trying to stop a killing. I'll read the report later with you. Call Meeks and inform him I'm back in Bellingham to help if I can," Dick explained as he put on his jacket to leave.

"Can do, where are you going now." Marty asked?

"I'm headed for Skylark Restaurant where Bass works. I'll ask for any help. The law needs to find Ping before he can get to Tweed or Me Li."

At the restaurant, Dick found Bass wiping down the counter and asked to talk for a minute, "It's about Tweed's life," Dick said.

Bass immediately became upset and asked, "What do you mean Tweed's life?"

"I mean, a man is in Bellingham to find and kill Tweed and Me Li because the Chinese Red Army wants them dead."

"They know too much and failed to accomplish their jobs," Dick explained.

"Why are you worried? They're both in jail, and the man can't get to them."

"Don't be so sure. This man Ping is a trained spy and killer. He can get to almost anybody if he needs to," Dick stated.

"What can I do," Bass asked?

"Just keep your eyes open for an Asian man like this one." Dick showed a picture of Ping to Bass on his cell phone. "Let me know if you see him, and I will come with the police," Dick explained.

"Sure, I can do that."

Dick went back to his car and called Meeks for any information he could get from Me Li about Ping's routines and habits and way of thinking.

"Dick! What's up?"

"Hi, Meeks, will you go to Me Li's cell and ask her if Ping was familiar with Bellingham and if he has friends here or in Canada? Tell her Ping has come to kill her and Tweed before he goes back to China," Dick asked?

"I'll talk to her and get back to you," Meeks responded.

Dick was now on a manhunt while Agent Warren watched over Susan.

With Chung dead, Ping had no place to go. Then Dick remembered Chung's boat.

Dick found Chung's boat secured to a buoy in Bellingham Bay at Fairhaven, where the sheriff's department had left it after they were finished investigating it.

Dick was able to rent a small boat at a boat rental shop and row out toward Chung's boat, "Cyclops."

As Dick rowed closer to Cyclops, he noticed the stern passage door on the bulwark was swaying to the rhythm of the lazy swells.

He stopped rowing, looked over the boat, and pulled his revolver to check the ammo.

Dick continued to row toward the boat, watching closely for any movement. Soon, he was at the stern of Cyclops and tied off his rowboat. An eerie feeling came over him as he looked at the dead boat. He could see blood on the bulwark rail and the Salone door partly open. He glanced up at the bridge and it was clear. He continued onto the swim step, up the stern ladder, and onto the deck.

He slowly walked through the open door leading into the salon and he noticed blood on the floor leading up the passageway to the pilothouse.

Fear ran through him at the sight of a woman's body on the deck, face down. She had been shot in the back of the head. Dick felt her neck, it was cold with no pulse. He lifted the woman's head to see Chung Young Yi. Shocked, the sight of the young student overwhelmed him.

He sat down in the captain's chair to catch his breath and compose himself before calling Steven to report the death of this innocent young lady on Cyclops.

Ping must have seen her talking to me at the university, come into the room after I left and forced her with him. He brought her to Bellingham and killed her on the boat, Dick thought to himself.

Dick stood over the young lady, feeling very heavy, sad, and angry about getting her killed. His heart was sad knowing this young lady had stepped into a cruel world of evil and met Satan.

Dick walked out on the stern of the boat, sat on a settee and called Warrant Officer Steven to inform him what he had found.

Within minutes, a coast guard boat came alongside and secured to the port side of the Cyclops. The crew came aboard to secure the crime scene.

Once aboard, Steven contacted Dick as he sat at the stern of the boat, asked how he was doing and whether he needed some time to compose himself before talking.

"I'm okay, I feel awful about this lady getting killed because of me. Let's get on with it and find the son of a bitch that killed her," Dick demanded.

After their conversation, Steven had one crewman take Dick's rented boat back to the rental shop, and the CG boat towed Cyclops to the station for the investigators and coroner to do their work.

Back at the station, Steven said, "You know who killed her, and you believe he is in Bellingham. What are you going to do?"

"I'll call Meeks to inform him about what I found on Cyclops and start my search for Ping," Dick responded.

"Take care, and let me know if I can help," Steven said as Dick got into a CG pickup for a ride back to Fairhaven and his car.

After Dick arrived back at his car, he drove to Fairhaven boatyard to see if Ping was there. He didn't find Clinton's car and decided to recheck the warehouse for Ping or Clinton.

The last time I went into this warehouse, I got knocked on the head, thought Dick as he pulled his revolver out and entered the hollow dim-lit building. He walked slowly, pointing his revolver into the dark corners of the building. The main floor was clear, and he headed for the second floor.

Dick eased up the staircase one squeaking step at a time until he was at the top. He moved down the hallway, checking each room as he advanced. Suddenly, all went dark.

Dick blinked his eyes to clear his vision and rubbed the back of his head. *Damn it! Ping hit me again,* thought Dick as he stood up, holding onto the wall to steady himself.

He quickly scanned the room for his revolver and spotted it in the middle of the room. *Ping knows he can't take any weapon to Canada; that's why he left it.*

Dick called Steven to advise him that Ping may try to steal a boat to use to get to Canada. Steven said he would advise the harbormaster and start the search for Ping.

CHAPTER 19

THE TEAM CLOSES IN

Realizing Ping had a huge head start and was probably on the water for Canada, Dick headed back to the office to fill in Marty on what had happened while the coast guard searched among the hundreds of islands in the archipelago.

As Dick walked through the office door, he didn't see Marty. "Marty, are you in here?"

"Yes, I'm in the bathroom, I'll be out just as soon as I wash the blood off my hands," Marty shouted back.

What the hell does she mean wash the blood off her hands? Dick thought as he started walking toward the bathroom door.

At that moment, Marty came out of the bathroom, drying her hands with a paper towel.

"What the hell happened?"

"The aid unit just left with Bass. They took him to the hospital; he was shot," explained Marty.

"Who shot him?"

"I don't know. He staggered into the office and fell to the floor. He was unconscious," Marty responded.

"Ping is killing off anyone connected to his operation," Dick explained to Marty.

"So Ping shot Bass?"

"I believe he did. There isn't anyone else wanting to kill Bass. I've got to call Meeks and tell him about this," Dick said as he picked up the phone.

After the phone call, Dick said, "Marty, all we can do now is wait for the county sheriff or the coast guard to find Ping.

I have one more call to make. I have to call David to find out how Susan is doing."

After a five-minute conversation with David, Dick hung up feeling good about Susan's health and said to Marty, "Susan is doing fine and will be out of the hospital soon."

The day was finally good for Dick after the phone call. Now he waited for a call from Steven or Meeks telling him they had Ping.

At daybreak Dick's phone rang, waking him. He answered, "What's up, Steven?"

"This morning a boat owner was loading his boat for a trip at the Squalicum Marina. While loading his cart, he propped open the security gate and didn't notice a man walking past him and through the gate. This man boarded the owner's boat and took it. The owner called the station to report the theft."

"What kind of a boat was it?"

"It was a forty-five foot Bayliner by the name of Sand Piper. I'm getting underway to search for it. Would you like to go on a hunting trip, Dick," Steven asked?

"You bet your ass! I want to be there when you hook that bottom-feeder."

Before long, the forty-five-foot CG boat was cutting through the water, throwing up a rooster tail from its water jets. Steven was strapped in a seat searching the waters with his field glasses for the Bayliner."

Dick hung onto a handrail to keep his feet on the deck as the boat dropped over the crest of four-foot waves and crashed hard into the trough between the waves. The windshield wipers slaved to clear the water away.

The CC boat headed up Hale Passage, North, to the southeast side of Sucia Island where Steven noticed an eighty-seven-foot CG cutter secured to a buoy, standing watch for drug runners coming from Canada. He radioed the cutter for information about the stolen Bayliner.

The master chief of the cutter informed Steven that a forty-five-foot, white, Bayliner came out of the South, passed him and headed north onto Georgia Straights about twenty minutes ago. He was travelling at high speed.

"That's the boat," Steven responded back to the master chief.

Steven kept his crew driving hard around the northeast end of Sucia Island, onto the Georgia Straights and four-foot rolling seas.

"Do you see that boat up ahead, Steven," Dick asked?

"I see a white boat about two miles off. We should overtake it within a few minutes if these waves lay down," Steven responded.

As they approached the boat, they could see it wasn't a Bayliner and they veered off toward Patos Island to check out a cove tucked inside the island with a sandy beach; a great place to hide a boat.

The CG boat slowed to maneuvering speed and headed into the small island, ready to take the killer into custody, but they found the bay vacant. Then they headed for the west side of Sucia; to search out the small inlets and Fossil Bay.

"Ping may try to rent an airplane at Friday Harbor," Dick said.

"He may," Steven responded as he continued searching the waters through his field glasses. As the boat eased out of Fossil Bay, Steven suddenly became interested in a white boat moving into a small dock across the water on the north side of Orcas Island.

"This looks promising, there's a small airstrip on the north side of Orcas, close to the boat dock."

"Kick this boat in the ass, coxswain, we need to get there just in case Ping is heading for a plane," Steven shouted!

The CG boat sped across the water to the small dock. The coxswain slowed and maneuvered alongside the dock, securing behind a white Bayliner.

Two crew members stayed to secure the area. Two other crew went with Steven and Dick in search of Ping at the airstrip.

As the four ran past the Bayliner the hatch covers blew off the engine space, and flames engulfed it, roaring upward.

"The search for Ping will have to stop, we've got to get this fire under control," Steven shouted!

The crew and Steven fought the fire for half an hour to bring it under control and pumped water out to keep the boat afloat.

While Steven and the crew were occupied, Dick raced toward the airport.

The CG crew stayed back to make sure of the safety of the public and help the Orcas fire department.

"I'm going to help Dick," Steven said to his crew.

"Sure, go ahead. Ping is probably at the airstrip trying to rent or steal a plane.

Take this radio for Dick for immediate communications to the crew if he needs help," the coxswain said, handing Steven a CG radio.

By now, Dick had run down the dock and up the ramp to a sheriff's vehicle. He shouted to the officer, "Take me to the airstrip, I'm after a killer."

The patrol unit sped off, with Dick, toward the small unattended airstrip.

Upon arrival, Dick searched the short, two rows of planes anchored to the sides of the strip as the officer drove slowly along.

At the end of the strip, the officer stopped and looked at Dick. "What do you want to do now, sir," he asked?

"Stop, I want to check out that building over there at the end of the strip. That building looks like a general maintenance building for planes. That is a place Ping could hide," Dick explained.

"Sure, I'll park over to the other side and watch to make sure no one comes in on you and watch for Ping coming out," the deputy assured Dick.

Dick ran up to the building door and stood with his revolver at the ready. He listened for any activity inside. All seemed quiet.

Dick slowly opened one of the doors and peeked inside. All was still quiet. Dick dove inside the building toward a table. Suddenly a shot rang out; hot lead bore into Dick's left leg, stunning him. He rolled, painfully, under a steel work table. With no time to lose, he ripped his shirt sleeve off and wrapped it around his leg to stop the bleeding.

Before he could do anything else, another shot rang out and dirt sprayed up beside him, and into his face. Realizing he could not stay there, he rolled out from under the table as he fired at the muzzle flash coming from a loft above.

All went silent. Dick had tumbled behind a racked engine. It gave him time to tighten the sleeve on his leg and reload his revolver.

The bleeding stopped.

Dick began searching the loft for Ping.

"Ping! Give it up, the police are outside, and you will die if you don't," Dick shouted!

Again, all was silent.

"Ping! Give it up! Throw out your gun and come out," Dick shouted out again.

Dick could hear a patrol car siren sounding off in the distance.

"Ping! Can you hear that police car coming! You don't have a chance, unless you give up to me," Dick shouted!

By now, most of the sheriff's department assigned to Orcas Island had arrived outside of the building.

"Ping! Can you hear the police outside ready to come in! If they come in, you will surely die!" Dick shouted again.

All was quiet. Suddenly, a dove broke the silence by flying out a loft window.

Surprisingly, Ping made his move. "Don't shoot, I'm coming out!"

With an urge to shoot Ping, Dick held his gun toward the loft until he could see if Ping was truly coming out.

By this time, Officer Steven had arrived at Dick's location and shouted out, "I'm outside the door!"

"Okay, Ping," Dick said, "Come on out, the deputies will hold their gunfire! No one will shoot."

At this point, Ping thought over his options: if he was sent back to China, the army would shoot him for his inability to keep his cover and do his job. If he gave up, the US Courts would put him in prison for life, where he would be killed by some redneck.

Ping shouted out, "I'm coming down, don't shoot." He threw down his gun and climbed down from the loft. Once on the floor,

Ping turned, swung his Uzi up and started firing bullets toward the location of Dick.

The shop door flung open. Two deputies and Steven fired in unison at Ping, now standing in the middle of the building.

The Uzi dropped from Ping's hands. He smiled and stared at the ceiling as he dropped to his knees. For a moment, Ping stared at Dick, then fell forward landing face down on the dirty, oily, floor. Dark blood seeped out from under him.

"This assassin will never kill again," Steven stated.

"This has been one hell of a day, Officer Steven," Dick stated as he fell to the floor.

Steven looked at Dick lying on the floor; blood covered his shirt. "Shit! Dick's bleeding badly!"

Steven dropped to his knees, grabbed an oily rag and pressed it against Dick's bleeding chest.

"Seaman Yates, call Port Angeles for a helicopter to get Dick out of here to Saint Joseph's Hospital. Be quick about it."

Within a minute, the coast guard helicopter landed on the end of the airstrip, waiting to receive Dick.

Seaman Yates and his team had Dick in a lift basket in seconds and the helicopter lifted off to the hospital.

"How did the helo get here so quickly," a deputy asked?

"The helicopter was training in the area. The pilot watched the boat fire and listened to the action. Knowing some help would be needed, the helicopter stood by," Yates said.

Steven watched the helo go out of sight, then said, "Okay, men, let's head back to the boat and get back to the station. The deputies will handle Ping's body and the reports."

C H A P T E R   2 0

———————

WHAT'S NEXT?

For the rest of the day, there was no information on Dick's condition. Officer Steven could only find out that the coast guard helo transferred Dick to the ER hospital, barely alive. The crew believed it was a possibility Dick would not make it because of the large loss of blood.

Two days went by with little news on Dick's condition.

In the meantime, Susan was released from the hospital and was staying at Dick's house so she could be there when he was released.

Back at the hospital, again, Susan wasn't able to find out the facts about Dick. The doctors would only say he would recover.

Susan left, she realized she needed to hear Dick's story before she could finish her report.

That afternoon, Susan was at Meeks's office to find out what had happened on the day Dick was shot and Ping was killed. She received a copy of Meeks's reports, and later that day, she picked up a report from Warrant Officer Steven.

The following day, Susan was hard at work when she got a call from Steven telling her he was at the hospital when Dick woke up and that Dick could possibly talk to her tomorrow.

That information gave Susan a desire to finish her reports and turn them over to her boss while asking for a week off to rest from this investigation.

Her boss gave her time off for a job well done. She had cleared up an NSA case and shut down a spy ring. Her boss said she needed one more report to close the case of Chung Me Li.

He said she must make sure who formed the spy ring and all the spies were gone.

Susan agreed with her boss, and said she would interview Chung Me Li one more time, as soon as she could, and send him that report.

Early the next morning, Susan called to ask Dick's doctor when she could come and see Dick.

The doctor handed Dick the phone and said, "Here, Dick, talk to Susan." Dick took the phone and said, "Susan, come now." He needed to find out how she was doing after her release from the hospital and get an update on her case.

This was a happy day for the two of them, until the doctor told them Dick had to rest one more day before Susan could interview him.

Susan agreed.

Later, Susan called Meeks to explain that she needed to interview Chung Me Li to clear up a question on who started the spy operations and also make sure the operations were gone.

Meeks agreed to interview Chung Me Li the next day at ten o'clock.

The following day, at ten o'clock, Susan walked into Meeks's office, ready to do the interview of Me Li.

Meeks asked Susan if she was ready for her interview.

"Let's do it and get this case over," Susan commented.

Meeks and Susan walked into the interview room where Chung was waiting.

"Good morning, Mrs. Chung, are you ready to talk with Susan and me one more time?"

"Yes, I am," Chung stated.

At that point, Detective Meeks told Chung that Susan needed to question her about Dr. Ping. Then she could turn her case over to the US Marshal's Office.

Susan looked into Chung's eyes and said, "Me Li, the CIA has informed the FBI that the Red Army believed Chung failed in setting up a spy ring and had him killed. The CIA believed the Red Army had given the job to you."

Chung thought for a minute, *I know the control of the Red Army and that the CIA knows the truth,* "I'll do my best," she said.

"I need you to answer the question pertaining to who set up and ran the spy operation," Susan explained.

"Yes, I can give you that," Chung responded.

"Mrs. Chung, please start with who you are and who you work for and please don't lie for your sake," Susan said.

"First, I would like to ask something off the record," Chung stated.

"Sure," Susan said as she turned off the recorder.

"If I tell you what I know, the Chinese will not stop hunting for me. Can you protect me to a reasonable degree," Chung asked?

"Yes. The US Marshal's Office will take you into their protection program and change your life," Susan said as she turned the recorder on.

"Okay, when I started working for the Chinese Army they sent me to a Red Army training center. Later, I was sent to a section of assassination and spying. At my graduation, I was considered a top assassin," Me Li explained.

"What did the Red Army do with you after your training," Susan questioned?

"Being a new agent and none of the other countries spy agencies knew me, I was sent to the States married to Chung Lee Yu, who was an import/export operator. My main job was to organize a spy operation using Chinese students picked and trained by the Red Army and sent to the university," Me Li stated.

"Was this spy-building operations successful?"

"Yes, the university was given a lot of money to assist these students, so much money that the university didn't vet them. Without vetting and the students being well trained, the setup was easy.

There is one other action that helped build this spy operation. Before starting the spy operation, I was sent to university as a guest lector to recon the area and interview students before starting," She said.

"Now, my most important question is, who is Mr. Ping," Susan asked?

"Ping was an assassin sent by the Chinese Army, through Mexico, to protect the operation and its secrets," Me Li said.

"Did Ping kill Jamie and Bodie when they were camping on Orcas Island?"

"I was told by a message from China that Jamie had hacked into the Chinese Army computer in some way and found that China was setting up some operation in the Seattle area. She, Jamie, had to be eliminated."

"How did Ping kill her," Susan asked?

"Ping received an order to eliminate Jamie and he began stalking her to find a time and place to eliminate her. The place was Orcas Island and with her friend on a camping trip. Ping followed them to Doe Bay. He got them up and walked them to the water's edge. He tied them in a way that the general public would believe they committed suicide as a love pact. He shot them with a .22 and pushed their bodies into the bay. He stayed the night in their tent and left the next morning for the ferry."

"Now that we have cleared up the killing of Jamie and Bodie, what about Chung," Meeks asked?

"Ping received orders to assassinate Chung due to his talking to unknown people in Mexico. They were not sure about him. Ping went to Chung's home and told him to go back to China and clear up questions. Chung refused, Ping shot him and left the house," Me Li explained.

"Who was the man killed in the warehouse the night Private Detective Dickson Diamond was beaten up?"

"He was Ping's assistant from China. He came into the States through Mexico at the same time as Ping," Me Li explained.

"The last killing we know of is a young student at the university. She was found on Chung's boat, shot in the head. Why did Ping kill her," Susan asked?

"Ping was at the university to meet Susan to kill her. She was getting too close to finding out about the spy operations.

Later Ping remembered he forgot to check to make sure Susan was dead and he went back. That was a big mistake for a trained assassin. He started to enter the building when he noticed a man going into the department. At this point, he had to hide in a clean-up cart. While in the cart, he overheard the young student talking to that man. When the man left, Ping grabbed the girl at gunpoint, forced her to his car, and took her to Bellingham, where he killed her. That is what Ping reported to me," Chung Me Li stated. "Now, I think I have told you what you wanted to hear."

"Yes, you have, you have covered all the killings. Now you will have to work with the court recorder to put your statement on record, then the US Marshal's Office will place you in the Federal Protective Service," Susan advised.

"I have one more item of the greatest interest for you, but I'm going to hold it back until I'm assured of safety in the States," Me Li said.

Meeks called and asked the prosecutors if they were finished with Me Li.

"Yes, until we hear from the US Marshal's office," They said.

With the interview over, Susan left the room wondering what else Me Li had to tell them.

"We will have to hold off for now," Meeks stated.

The next morning, Susan went to the hospital to see how Dick was doing. To her surprise, the doctor said Dick was up and asked for something to eat. The doctor also told Susan that Dick's blood was restored, and his wounds were healing. He would be out of the hospital in a day or so.

This was great news for Susan to hear and she asked how long she could talk to Dick.

"You can talk to him as long as he likes," the doctor responded.

Susan lost no time heading to Dick's room. She walked in to find Dick sitting up in bed. She said nothing to him; she walked over and gave him a big hug.

Dick said, "I love your hug, but you're putting a little too much pressure on my bullet holes."

Susan quickly released Dick, smiled a big smile, and said, "I'm so happy to see you have recovered, now we can take another ride up to Mount Baker."

"You bet we can. But for now, I'm stuck here, and the only excitement I can get is for you to hug me and update me on your spy case," Dick commented.

Susan said she would only tell Dick the ending of her spy case, and when he was out of the hospital, she'd tell him everything.

"Okay, I can live with that. Tell me what happened?"

For the next thirty minutes Susan told Dick the ending of her case while Dick laid back on his pillow.

When Susan had finished with her story she said it was time for her to go. She was going to spend her day at the coast guard station finishing up her reports for her boss.

Susan said goodbye while hugging him lightly.

Dick laid back on the bed, contemplated his release tomorrow and getting back to work with Marty.

CHAPTER 21

OUT AND ABOUT FOR DICK

Unbeknownst to Susan, Dick was released from the hospital that afternoon, at his insistence. He didn't call Susan because he wanted to surprise her.

Back home, Dick was having his usual TV dinner with a cold beer when the doorbell rang.

Now that the spies were eliminated, Dick felt safe, "Come in, the door's unlocked!"

Susan walked in with a bottle of wine declaring, "I came over to celebrate your being home."

"How did you know I was home?"

"I called the hospital to see when you would be released tomorrow and they said you were released this afternoon.

Why didn't you call me and tell me you were home?"

"I wanted to come home and rest up a little so we could have a good time together when we did meet," Dick explained.

"I'm sorry I wasn't there when you got out of the hospital, but that was sweet of you to surprise me," Susan sighed, warmly.

"I was just having another special dinner, would you like a TV dinner," Dick asked?

"No thanks, I knew you would offer me a TV dinner when I came over, so I had a quick sandwich at a fancy restaurant."

Dick grinned, "Have a seat, give me the wine and I'll open it.

My goodness, Susan, you bought an expensive bottle of wine. You must have paid at least five bucks for that," Dick teased as he unscrewed the bottle cap.

"I didn't want to spend out of your class," Susan responded with a happy laugh.

"Let's drink this reserved wine to the elimination of Ping, the wine fits him: deadly, cheap, and fortified," Dick said as he raised his glass.

They tipped their glasses and had a sip.

"My God, this wine is awful," Susan said, setting down the glass.

Dick asked, "What do you think about Ping being a cold-hearted killer and probably trained from childhood to kill?"

"I think he had orders to kill anyone, and like a machine, he did his job; Protect the spy ring," Susan commented.

"Do you think Me Li is the controller of the spy operations," Dick asked?

"I'm not sure, but Me Li seemed to have the overall knowledge," Susan said.

"I'm with you, I think the orders are coming straight from China by some kind of signals to Me Li," Dick said.

"I have the CIA working on that question. If China's Army is trying to run an operation here, the CIA and the FBI will find out and shut them down," Susan explained.

"I've got to go, Dick, I just wanted to stop by to have a drink with you. I've got to get back to the hotel and finish packing," Susan said as she stood up to leave.

"I'll see you tomorrow, Susan," Dick said as he walked her to the door.

"Remember, Me Li will be giving her surprise item tomorrow. If you are well enough to come for the interview, I'll see you there," Susan said.

"I'll be there. Her statement will close the curtains on China's spying in the Puget Sound for now," Dick responded.

The next day at nine o'clock, all parties were ready to hear what Me Li's surprise comments would be, before the US Marshal's Office took her.

In the interview room, Me Li sat and listened to the plan the Marshal's Office laid out, and she agreed with their plan to relocate her.

"Now, you want to know for sure who the great Red Army sent to set up the spy operation. I was the person setting up the operation. Second, Ping was sent to me as my protector. Thirdly, the calls to Mexico were to a man sending messages to and from China. Now, the part you don't know is the director of Chinese studies at the university was my boss and liaison with the export guy in Mexico. He was the direct contact with the Red Army. There was to be no contact between the Red Army and the spy operations throughout the States," Chung Me Li stated with confidence.

Susan excused herself and walked out onto the parking lot and called her boss and asked for information on Chung Me Li of the Chinese Army. Susan then returned to the interview room to proceed with the interview.

At noon, Me Li was taken back to her cell, and the others went to lunch.

At the restaurant, Marty asked Susan if she believed Me Li.

"Yes, I do because the marriage for Chung was too fast. I found China gave the U of W Chinese school of studies a huge grant. This grant was to help support a student and Ping, who was a visiting lector at the U of W. The money was so big that Ping's papers and certificates were never vetted. But I was totally surprised about the director of Chinese studies being the boss and liaison," Susan explained.

"What's next, Susan," Dick asked?

"We have to wait until I hear from the CIA about who Chung Me Li is, and the FBI will start an investigation into the school of Chinese studies. But that is my business, you or the sheriff don't have to worry about it," Susan stated.

Marty looked at her watch and said, "It's time for us to return to the interview and see what else Me Li has to say."

Susan went to the interview with Meeks while Dick and Marty watched from the viewing room.

The rest of the interview was non-productive for Susan until Me Li said, "The last item I have to say is that the man in Mexico is the man building a spy operation in a lot of universities across the States. The Seattle operation is only one of them."

"What in the hell are you talking about? Spies in our universities," Susan blurted out!

"That's right, Susan. If you are in doubt, have your CIA check it out," Chung Me Li stated with confidence.

At this point, Susan said she was finished.

Meeks agreed to finish the interview and sent Me Li back to her cell.

At two in the morning, Susan was awakened by a phone ringing in her hotel room. Answering, "Yes," she said as she looked at the clock on the nightstand. After a long pause she said, "Thanks."

At eight in the morning, Susan called Dick and asked him to meet her in the hotel restaurant for breakfast as she had something to tell him. She'd be there at nine-thirty.

At nine-thirty, they were having coffee in the Hotel Bellwether Restaurant, where Susan told Dick about the phone call at two AM from the CIA. They had received a response from their operatives in China, who found Major Chung Me Li in the Chinese Army, and she was nowhere to be found. The operatives believed she was in the U.S., forming some kind of secret operations. The CIA also said that Me Li is in the ranks of worldwide spies.

"Well, halleluiah! The CIA has confirmed Me Li's testimony," Dick proclaimed!

After their breakfast, Susan and Dick headed to the sheriff's office, in separate cars, to set up a time to see Chung Me Li turned over to the U.S. Marshal's Office.

Susan told Meeks, Dick, and Marty that she would turn over her report to the Federal Marshal's Office and they would decide what would happen to Me Li.

"Thanks, Susan, I think I can close out the killings of Jamie and Bodie's case and turn it over to the county prosecutor along with advising the Bellingham Police on our progress."

"I will update Peggy on our findings, and I believe that will close my case with her," Dick stated.

"Thanks, Susan, for all you have done to help in these investigations and forcing us to keep pushing for the right ending of Jamie's death, which led us to a huge spy operation here in the Puget Sound," Meeks said.

At this point, the two groups departed the sheriff's office and headed to their own offices.

Susan went to the coast guard station. There, she could have a private office to work, along with a federal law enforcement computer system and federal prosecutors.

Back in the office, Dick told Marty that instead of phoning Peggy, he was going to her home to give her their report. Then he was going home.

Marty said, "I will have another case ready for the two of us tomorrow."

CHAPTER 22

THE END IS NEAR

At home, Dick was having a good pizza, not his usual TV dinner with beer. The doorbell rang; Dick walked over and opened the door to see Susan standing with a folder for him.

"Come in and have pizza with me. I know you came over just to have pizza, right," Dick suggested.

"Sure, I knew you would be celebrating the closing of your case. I also came over to give you my report. You will keep it to yourself and tell no one. I will be leaving tomorrow."

"Tomorrow!" Dick responded.

"Yes, there is a conference with my boss. He has called a committee on spying in the U.S., and I will be the main speaker at that meeting," Susan said.

"My God! That was quick. I thought you would be here until the court trial was over," Dick exclaimed!

"No, I have another job waiting on me in DC. When I'm needed for the court here in San Juan County, I will come back. I'll see you then," Susan said.

"Now that we are not partners and not working on a case, we can sleep together," Dick said with a sly, grin.

"Not tonight, big boy," Susan responded smirking as she gave Dick a big hug and passionate kiss. Then, not saying a word, she headed out the door.

Dick stood there, stunned, and watched her leave.

Early the next morning, Susan left the hotel for the Bellingham International Airport and her trip back to FBI headquarters.

At the airport, Susan went over her files to prepare herself for her upcoming report.

Dick walked up, eased down beside her and said, "How about a date, pretty woman?"

"What are you doing here, Dick?"

"I just wanted to see you off, that's the right thing to do for a friend," Dick explained.

"That's a really sweet thing to do, Dick. I will always remember those little things you did for me and all the things we did together. Sit and talk while I wait for the plane to load," She invited.

"Susan, I wanted you to know, you have unchained me from my wife. You have awakened my dead feeling. It took your company to free me from the past," Dick expounded.

At that moment, the intercom announced, "The flight to Seattle is loading. Passengers, please line up to board."

"Goodbye, Dick, I'll be seeing you in my dreams," Susan commented as she stood up and hugged Dick, then walked toward the boarding door, pulling her rolling case behind her.

"Goodbye, Susan," Dick responded in a whisper as he stood, watched her walk out of his life, and wondered if he would ever see her again.

Suddenly, Dick's phone rang. "Hi, Dick here."

"Dick, this is Marty, there is a lady in the office wanting to hire us to find her missing daughter."

"I'm on my way." *Please God, not another brandy-drinking little old lady*, Dick thought as he headed back to his car and on to another adventure.

The End.

Maybe?

THE AUTHOR

I started my life as any kid did, Ernest Salotti thought. The ups and downs and confusion, except for having no father, a broken home, and traveling from address to address that finally forced Ernest into searching for a better life.

On his seventeenth birthday, his mother agreed to sign for him to join the army and save him from a bad future. The year was 1958. After that date, he spent most of his life with the army, coast guard, and law enforcement until retiring in 1999.

After retiring, he and his wife worked with the coast guard aux-iliary for fifteen years until they retired. Within that fifteen years, Ernest and his wife also traveled around the States, and Ernest started painting and writing.

www.ingramcontent.com/pod-product-compliance
Lightning Source LLC
Chambersburg PA
CBHW060334310726
48976CB00007B/2553